愛倫坡

MYSTERY SHORT STORIES OF EDGAR ALLAN POE

短篇小說選

原著 _ Edgar Allan Poe　改寫 _ Janet Olearski　譯者 _ 李璞良

ABOUT THIS BOOK

For the Student

 Listen to the story and do some activities on your Audio CD.

 Talk about the story.

For the Teacher

Go to our Readers Resource site for information on using readers and downloadable Resource Sheets, photocopiable Worksheets, and Tapescripts. www.helblingreaders.com

For lots of great ideas on using Graded Readers consult Reading Matters, the Teacher's Guide to using Helbling Readers.

Structures

Modal verb would	Non-defining relative clauses
I'd love to . . .	Present perfect continuous
Future continuous	Used to / would
Present perfect future	Used to / used to doing
Reported speech / verbs / questions	Second conditional
Past perfect	Expressing wishes and regrets
Defining relative clauses	

Structures from other levels are also included.

CONTENTS

Edgar Allan Poe was born on January 19th 1809 in Boston, Massachusetts, USA. His parents died when he was just two years old, and he was brought up[1] by John Allan, a Scottish businessman.

Poe was educated in Britain and the US. He was a good student and he attended the University of Virginia, and the famous West Point Military Academy. Poe spent two years in the army and in this period he completed his first two collections of poetry, published in 1827 and 1829.

Poe worked as a journalist and critic with several magazines and newspapers. He wrote many short stories including *The Murders in the Rue Morgue* (1841), *The Pit and the Pendulum* (1843) and *The Black Cat* (1843). These

stories dealt with[2] dark, disturbing[3] themes and in America Poe was criticized for his 'Gothic[4]' writing style. In Europe, however, his work was popular and influential.

Poe suffered from illness and depression. The deaths of several close family members including his young wife Virginia affected him deeply. To alleviate[5] his depression Poe drank heavily, but this caused health problems. His writing earned him little money, and he lived in poverty, accumulating debts. He died on October 7th 1849.

Poe's major contribution to world literature was the development of the short story as an art form.

1 bring up 長大
2 deal with 處理
3 disturbing [dɪs`tɝbɪŋ] (a.) 使心神不寧的
4 Gothic [`gɑθɪk] (a.) 氣氛詭異的哥德式小說的
5 alleviate [ə`livɪˌet] (v.) 減輕；緩和

THE FALL OF THE HOUSE OF USHER

ABOUT THE BOOK

The three stories in this collection, **The Fall of the House of Usher**, **The Oval Portrait**, and **The Masque of the Red Death** are examples of short stories in the 'Gothic' tradition. Gothic literature became popular in Britain in the late 18th century and it explores the dark side of human nature and experience: death, ghosts, alienation[1], depression, madness[2] and desolate[3] settings. Poe brought Gothic literature to America. The atmosphere created by Poe in each of these stories is one of both physical and psychological fear and horror. Recurrent[4] themes in the stories are madness and death.

---

1 alienation [ˌeljəˈneʃən] (n.) 疏遠；離間
2 madness [ˈmædnɪs] (n.) 瘋狂
3 desolate [ˈdɛslɪt] (a.) 絕望的；悽慘的
4 recurrent [rɪˈkɜ˙ənt] (a.) 一再發生的
5 feature [ˈfitʃɚ] (n.) 特徵；特色
6 troubled [ˈtrʌbl̩d] (a.) 苦惱的
7 demented [dɪˈmɛntɪd] (a.) 精神錯亂的
8 bury [ˈbɛrɪ] (v.) 埋葬

The Fall of the House of Usher was written in 1839. It is one of Poe's most popular horror stories and contains all the essential features[5] of a Gothic story: a frightening house, a desolate landscape, a mysterious illness, stormy weather and troubled[6] characters. The story, which tells of the demented[7] Roderick Usher and his strange twin sister, Lady Madeline, is now regarded as a classic short story masterpiece.

Poe creates a sense of claustrophobia in the story. The characters cannot move freely within the house. And the narrator cannot escape until the house physically collapses. Madeline and Roderick are twins and this stops them from developing as full individuals. Madeline is buried[8] while she is still alive and she finally kills her brother by falling on him and crushing him.

The story has inspired many other works including films, operas, plays, popular music, computer games and numerous works of fiction.

1 Look at these scenes from *The Fall of the House of Usher*. Discuss with a partner.

a) Write at least 5 words or phrases to describe each scene.
b) What is the atmosphere like in each one?
c) What is happening in each scene?

2 Working in groups of three or four, look at the pictures and your descriptions once more. Together write two or three sentences to describe what you think will happen in the story. Compare your summary with those of the other groups in the class.

3 You may find this story and the others in this book very frightening. Or perhaps nothing frightens you! Work with a partner. Describe your scariest experience, or something you heard or saw that made you feel afraid.

4 Irrational fears are also called phobias. Can you match these phobias with their meanings?

_____ ⓐ arachnophobia   ① fear of closed spaces
_____ ⓑ claustrophobia   ② fear of storms
_____ ⓒ brontophobia   ③ fear of dead things
_____ ⓓ agoraphobia   ④ fear of spiders
_____ ⓔ necrophobia   ⑤ fear of open spaces

5 What are you afraid of? Here are some of the things that make people feel afraid. How do they affect you? Rate them from 0 (not at all scary) to 5 (very scary).

_____ ⓐ bees and wasps
_____ ⓑ being on your own
_____ ⓒ exams
_____ ⓓ flying
_____ ⓔ going to the dentist
_____ ⓕ heights
_____ ⓖ lifts
_____ ⓗ the dark

6 Work with a partner and write sentences comparing how you both feel about the things above.

7 Listen to the opening of the story. Which of the sentences below best describes how the narrator feels? Tick (✓).

_____ ⓐ The narrator is looking forward to going to the House of Usher.
_____ ⓑ The narrator is indifferent to going to the House of Usher.
_____ ⓒ The narrator feels uneasy and unhappy about going to the House of Usher.

8 Read these sentences from the story. They all describe sounds. Then listen and match the underlined words with the sounds.

_____ a The suits of armor, which <u>rattled</u> as I walked were things which I remembered from my childhood.

_____ b The tapestries swayed fitfully to and fro making <u>rustling</u> noises about my bed.

_____ c Shaking off my fear with a <u>gasp</u>, I sat up against my pillows.

_____ d He lifted up his mace, and <u>cracked</u> and ripped the door, and tore everything apart.

_____ e Exactly as I had imagined the dragon's unnatural <u>shriek</u> to be.

_____ f There was the <u>breaking</u> open of her coffin, the <u>grating</u> of the iron hinges of her prison.

_____ g Then, with a <u>low moaning</u> cry, she fell heavily onto her brother.

_____ h The whirlwind gave a fierce <u>blast</u>.

9 Meet the three characters of the story. Look at the illustrations. Describe them. Invent as much detail as you can.

The Narrator

Roderick Usher

Madeline Usher

10 Here are some words that appear in the story.
Match them with the pictures.

_____ a armor   _____ e tapestry
_____ b coffin   _____ f tree trunk
_____ c lute   _____ g vault
_____ d shield   _____ h web

11 Use the words above to complete these sentences.

a Spirits danced happily around a king to the music of a
_____.
b A _____ of shining brass hung on the wall.
c Dark _____ hung on the wall.
d The branches of the dead _____ had once been
green with leaves.
e We opened the lid of the _____ and looked at
the face of its occupant.
f Minute fungi were hanging in a fine tangled
_____ from the edges of the roof.
g Suits of _____ stood in the corridors of the
house and rattled as I walked past.
h The _____ was small and damp, and did not
admit any light.

12 In the story you will read about someone who goes to visit
an old friend. Imagine that you go to visit a friend who you
haven't seen for a long time. Your friend has changed. Write
a short paragraph about the changes.

For a whole dull[1], dark, and soundless autumn day, when the clouds were low in the sky, I had been riding alone through the dreary[2] countryside. Eventually, as evening fell, I found myself within view of the melancholy House of Usher. When I saw the building, I felt a sense of gloom[3].

I looked at the scene before me – at the house and the simple landscape, at the bleak[4] walls, at the vacant eye-like windows, at the rough grass, and at a few white trunks of decayed[5] trees – with a sense of depression, like an opium addict awakening from his dream. I felt a sense of iciness and my heart felt cold and heavy. What was it that made me so nervous when I thought about the House of Usher? It was a mystery, and I could not fight against the dark thoughts that filled me.

PLACES

- Have you ever visited a place and suddenly felt happy or sad? Describe how you felt. Why did this place make you feel this way?
- Was it something to do with the weather, the appearance of the place, or the people who were there?

1 dull [dʌl] (a.) 陰沉的
2 dreary [ˋdrɪərɪ] (a.) 沉悶的；陰鬱的
3 gloom [glum] (n.) 陰鬱
4 bleak [blik] (a.) 荒涼的
5 decayed [dɪˋked] (a.) 腐朽的

I was forced to come to the unsatisfactory conclusion that some things are beyond our understanding. If the scene in front of me had been arranged in any different way it possibly would not have left me with such a sad impression. With this in mind, I rode my horse to the edge of a black lake that was close to the house and, trembling more than before, I looked down on the reflection of the grey grass, the ghastly[1] tree trunks, and the empty eye-like windows in the water.

Nevertheless, I was proposing to stay a few weeks in this gloomy house. Its owner, Roderick Usher, had been one of my childhood companions, but it had been many years since our last meeting. A letter from him had reached me, and it gave evidence that he was very disturbed. The writer spoke of physical illness, and of a disorder of the mind. He said I was his best and only friend, and he felt that the cheerfulness of my company would lessen[2] his malady[3]. I did not hesitate when I read this. I obeyed his request immediately.

RODERICK USHER

- How does the narrator know Roderick Usher?
- Why does Usher write to the narrator?
- What does Usher ask the narrator to do?

1 ghastly [ˈgæstlɪ] (a.) 如鬼魅的
2 lessen [ˈlɛsn̩] (v.) 減緩
3 malady [ˈmælədɪ] (n.) 痼疾
4 reserved [rɪˈzɜˇvɪd] (a.) 緘默的
5 I was aware 我知道
6 produce [prəˈdjus] (v.) 繁衍
7 branch [bræntʃ] (n.) 旁系後代
8 direct line of descent 一脈相傳的嫡系

14

Although, as boys, we had been quite close, I knew very little about my friend. He had always been very reserved . I was aware , however, that his family had displayed its talent over the years in many works of art. They had also performed repeated acts of charity, as well as showing passionate devotion to music. I learned too that, for the most part, the Usher family had never produced any continuing branch . And that the entire family was in a direct line of descent . Indeed this had always been the case with very little variation.

The Noble and Ancient House of
USHER

Alfred Usher m. Meredith Taylor

James   Richard m. Anne Barley   Catherine

Susan   Beth   Roger m. Eliza Preston   Anne

Madeline   Roderick

I began to think about how the character of the house perfectly matched[1] the character of the people who lived in it, and I speculated[2] on the possible influence that, over the centuries, the one might have exercised[3] on the other. Indeed it was this lack[4] of descendants, and the continual passing down[5] from father to son of the family home along with the family name, which had eventually caused both to be identified with the title of the estate[6]: the 'House of Usher'. In the minds of the peasantry[7] who used it, this title seems to include both the family and the family mansion[8].

FAMILY

- What do we know about the Usher family? Tick the correct answers.
  - ☐ Roderick has got a large extended family.
  - ☐ Roderick's family are interested in the arts.
  - ☐ Roderick's family inherited the house recently.
  - ☐ The Usher family has always been small.
- Now think of your own family. How far can you trace your family tree?

1 perfectly matched 非常地相稱
2 speculate [ˈspɛkjəˌlet] (v.) 思索；推測
3 exercise [ˈɛksɚˌsaɪz] (v.) 行使
4 lack [læk] (n.) 缺乏
5 pass down 傳下來
6 estate [ɪsˈtet] (n.) 地產
7 peasantry [ˈpɛzn̩trɪ] (n.) 農民
8 mansion [ˈmænʃən] (n.) 大廈；宅第
9 concentrate [ˈkɑnsɛnˌtret] (v.) 專注

10 pestilent [ˈpɛstələnt] (a.) 有毒的
11 vapor [ˈvepɚ] (n.) 氣；煙霧
12 tangled [ˈtæŋɡl̩d] (a.) 糾結的
13 inconsistency [ˌɪnkənˈsɪstənsɪ] (n.) 不一致
14 crumbling [ˈkrʌmblɪŋ] (a.) 破敗的
15 perceptible [pɚˈsɛptəbl̩] (a.) 可察覺的
16 crack [kræk] (n.) 裂縫
17 valet [ˈvælɪt] (n.) 男僕
18 winding [ˈwaɪndɪŋ] (a.) 蜿蜒的

When I looked up again at the house itself, from its image in the water, a strange thought grew in my mind. It was a thought so ridiculous that I only say it to show the strength of the feelings that oppressed me. I had concentrated[9] so much on my imagination that I really believed there was an atmosphere around the whole house and surrounding area that had no connection with the air of heaven. This atmosphere seemed to come from the decayed trees, the grey wall, and the silent lake like a pestilent[10] and mysterious vapor[11].

Shaking off from my spirit what felt like a dream, I looked at the building in more detail. Its main feature seemed to be its excessive age. It was discolored, and tiny fungi covered the whole exterior, hanging in a fine tangled[12] web from the edges of the roof. There appeared to be some inconsistency[13] between the apparently perfect state of the bricks, and the crumbling[14] condition of the individual stones. Apart from this sign of extensive decay, the construction gave little sign of instability. Perhaps a careful observer might have discovered a barely perceptible[15] crack[16] extending from the roof of the building in front, and that zigzagged down the wall until it became lost in the waters of the lake.

Noticing these things, I rode over a short bridge to the house. A servant took my horse, and I entered the Gothic archway of the hall. A valet[17] led me, in silence, through many dark winding[18] corridors to his master's room. Much of what I saw on the way contributed to increase the feelings of which I have already spoken. The objects around me, the carvings on the ceilings, the dark tapestries on the walls, the black floors, and the suits of armor, which rattled as I walked, were all things which I remembered from my childhood.

Still, I was surprised at the unfamiliar thoughts that these ordinary images were creating in me. On one of the staircases, I met the physician[1] of the family. I thought he had a puzzled[2] expression on his face. He seemed agitated[3] and walked past me. The valet opened a door and accompanied me in to the presence of his master.

The room in which I found myself was very large and high. The windows were long and narrow, and at a vast distance from the black wooden floor, making them inaccessible[4] from inside the room. Feeble[5] rays of light filtered through the window panes[6], so that it was possible to see the more prominent objects; however, it was difficult to see the remoter corners of the room, or the ceiling. Dark tapestries hung on the walls. The furniture was old and tattered[7]. Many books and musical instruments lay scattered[8] about. I felt that I was breathing an atmosphere of sadness. An air of gloom pervaded[9] everything.

WARNING SIGNS

- Think about what the narrator has seen and thought so far. What signs are there to warn us that something is wrong in the House of Usher?

1 physician [fɪˋzɪʃən] (n.) 醫師
2 puzzled [ˋpʌzl̩d] (a.) 困惑的
3 agitated [ˋædʒə͵tetɪd] (a.) 激動的
4 inaccessible [͵ɪnækˋsɛsəbl̩] (a.) 達不到的
5 feeble [ˋfibl̩] (a.) 微弱的
6 pane [pen] (n.) 窗戶玻璃
7 tattered [ˋtætəd] (a.) 破爛的
8 scattered [ˋskætəd] (a.) 散落的
9 pervade [pəˋved] (v.) 瀰漫

When I entered, Usher rose from a sofa on which he had been lying, and greeted me warmly, but I thought he did so with exaggerated cordiality[1]. A glance[2] at his face, however, convinced me of his sincerity.

We sat down and for some moments I looked at him with a feeling half of pity, half of awe[3]. No man had changed so much in such a brief period as Roderick Usher had! It was with difficulty that I recognized as my childhood friend the pale man in front of me.

The features of his face had always been unique. He had the pale skin of a corpse[4], eyes that were large and luminous, and lips that were thin and very pale, but that had a beautiful shape. His nose was delicate, but with broad nostrils[5]. He had a finely shaped chin, and hair that had a web-like softness. These features, together with a wide forehead, made up a face that was not easily forgotten. Now his features were exaggerated, and everything about him was so different that I doubted that I was speaking to my friend. The paleness of the skin, and the shiny look of his eyes shocked me most of all. The silky hair, too, had grown long and wild, and it floated around his face. I could not, even with effort, think of him as someone normal.

1 cordiality [kɔr`dʒælətɪ] (n.) 誠摯
2 glance [glæns] (n.) 一瞥
3 awe [ɔ] (n.) 畏怯
4 corpse [kɔrps] (n.) 屍體
5 nostril [`nɑstrɪl] (n.) 鼻孔

I was struck by my friend's incoherence[1]. But I soon discovered that this came from his attempts to overcome[2] his nervousness. I had been prepared for this both from his letter and from my memory of certain physical and emotional characteristics he had had when he was a boy. One minute he was lively and the next he was quiet. His voice changed often, from being trembling and indecisive to sounding like the voice of someone who is drunk[3] or drugged[4].

He spoke about the purpose[5] of my visit, of his earnest[6] desire to see me, and of the comfort he expected to have from my presence. He talked at some length about what he believed to be the nature of his malady. It was, he said, a sickness that was in his family, and one for which he had lost hope of finding a remedy[7].

He immediately added that it was only a nervous complaint[8], which would undoubtedly go away soon. It showed itself in various unnatural sensations. Some of these interested and bewildered[9] me although this may have been because of the way he described them. He suffered from an acuteness[10] of the senses. He could only eat the most simple food and he could only wear clothes of a certain texture. He found the smell of all flowers oppressive, the smallest quantity of light tortured his eyes, and only a few sounds, mostly those from stringed instruments[11], did not fill him with horror.

---

1 incoherence [ˌɪnkoˈhɪrəns] (n.) 不連貫
2 overcome [ˌovɚˈkʌm] (v.) 克服
3 drunk [drʌŋk] (a.) 喝醉酒的
4 drugged [ˈdrʌgɪd] (a.) 嗑藥的
5 purpose [ˈpɝpəs] (n.) 目的
6 earnest [ˈɝnɪst] (a.) 懇切的
7 remedy [ˈrɛmədɪ] (n.) 治療法
8 complaint [kəmˈplent] (n.) 身體不適
9 bewilder [bɪˈwɪldɚ] (v.) 使迷惑
10 acuteness [əˈkjutnɪs] (n.) 敏銳

ILLNESS

- What are the outward signs of Usher's illness?
- Is there anything strange about his symptoms?
- What do you think is wrong with him? Is his illness real or imaginary? Write how his illness affects his senses.

He was a slave to an abnormal kind of terror. 'I shall die', he said, 'I *must* die because of this fear. Not for any other reason. I dread the events of the future. I have no fear of danger, but I feel that the time will arrive sooner or later when I will have to give up both my life and my reason in my struggle with this terrible FEAR.'

Little by little and through occasional hints, I learned another particular feature of his mental condition. He was obsessed by certain superstitious ideas about the house in which he lived, and which he had never left for many years. Over a long period of time the building with its grey walls and towers, and the dim lake into which they all looked, had gained control over his spirit.

---

11 stringed instrument 管絃樂器
12 dread [drɛd] (v.) 懼怕；擔心
13 give up 放棄
14 hint [hɪnt] (n.) 暗示

15 superstitious [ˌsupɚˋstɪʃəs] (a.) 迷信的
16 dim [dɪm] (a.) 暗淡的
17 gain [gen] (v.) 獲得

He admitted, with hesitation, that much of his sadness could be traced[1] to a more natural origin – to the severe and lengthy illness, indeed to the approaching death, of his much loved sister. His sister had been his only companion for many years and she was his last and only relative on earth. 'Her death', he said, with a bitterness[2] I can never forget, 'would leave me as the last of the ancient race of the Ushers.'

As he spoke, Lady Madeline (this was her name) passed slowly through a remote part of the room and disappeared without noticing me. I watched her with astonishment mixed with dread[3], and yet I found it impossible to explain these feelings. My eyes followed her as if I were in a trance[4]. When eventually a door closed behind her, I turned instinctively to look at her brother. He had buried his face in his hands, and I could see that an unusual whiteness had spread across his emaciated[5] fingers and through them many tears trickled[6].

Lady Madeline's disease had puzzled her doctors for a long time. Her unusual symptoms were apathy, a gradual wasting away[7] of her body, and frequent periods of falling into a deep sleep. Up to now she had coped[8] with her malady, and she had not stayed in her bed. But, on the evening of my arrival at the house, she gave in[9] to her illness (as her brother told me that night with great agitation). I knew that I would probably never see the lady alive again.

---

1 trace [tres] (v.) 追溯
2 bitterness ['bɪtərnəss] (n.) 痛苦
3 dread [drɛd] (n.) 懼怕
4 trance [træns] (n.) 恍惚
5 emaciated [ɪˈmeʃɪˌetɪd] (a.) 極瘦的
6 trickle [ˈtrɪkl] (v.) 徐徐流下
7 waste away 消瘦
8 cope [kop] (v.) 對付
9 give in 讓步

In the following days we did not mention her name again. During this period I was busy trying to lighten[1] my friend's mood[2]. We painted and read together, or I listened, as if in a dream, as he played his guitar. But as I grew closer to him I realized the futility of all my attempts to cheer[3] a mind that was full of darkness and gloom.

MOODS

- What activities does the narrator involve Usher in to cheer him up?
- What about you? If you feel sad or upset, what helps you to feel better? What do you do to change your mood?
- When you are sad do you like to see friends or do you prefer to be on your own?

I shall always remember the many solemn hours I spent alone like this with the master of the House of Usher. Yet I would not be able to explain the occupations in which he involved me. The dull music he improvised[4] will ring[5] forever in my ears. His paintings thrilled[6] me and filled me with awe with their vivid[7] images yet I could only understand a small part of their meaning. If ever a person painted an idea that person was Roderick Usher.

---

1 lighten [ˈlaɪtn̩] (v.) 使輕鬆
2 mood [mud] (n.) 心情
3 cheer [tʃɪr] (v.) 提振心情
4 improvise [ˈɪmprəvaɪz] (v.) 即席作曲或作詩
5 ring [rɪŋ] (v.) 響
6 thrill [θrɪl] (v.) 使震顫
7 vivid [ˈvɪvɪd] (a.) 生動的
8 source [sors] (n.) 來源
9 flood [flʌd] (n.) 大量

One of the ghostly pieces that my friend produced, which was less abstract than the rest, I can describe in words. A small picture showed the interior of a long, rectangular tunnel, with low smooth white walls. The picture conveyed the idea that this tunnel lay deep below the surface of the earth. There were no visible doors or openings, and no torch or other source of artificial light could be seen, yet a flood of intense rays filled the whole scene with inappropriate splendor.

I have already mentioned the condition of the auditory[10] nerve that made all music intolerable to the sufferer, except for certain notes played on stringed instruments. He had to confine himself to narrow limits on the guitar and this perhaps was the reason for his strange performances. However it does not explain the wild passion of the verbal improvisations he often used to accompany his guitar. I remember well the words of one of these rhapsodies[11]. Listening to him I had the impression that he was aware for the first time that he was going mad.

The verses, which were entitled 'The Haunted Palace', told of a wonderful palace full of jewels and fine things in which spirits danced happily around their king to the music of a lute[12]. The inhabitants of the palace sang songs in beautiful voices praising the wisdom[13] of their ruler. But then one day evil creatures entered the palace and killed the king. That was many years ago. Now travelers who are passing by and who look through the windows into the palace see ghosts dancing to a discordant[14] melody.

---

10 auditory [ˈɔdə͵torɪ] (a.) 聽覺的
11 rhapsody [ˈræpsədɪ] (n.) 狂詩
12 lute [lut] (n.) 琵琶
13 wisdom [ˈwɪzdəm] (n.) 智慧
14 discordant [dɪsˈkɔrdn̩t] (a.) 不和諧的

I well remember that discussions of this ballad[1] led us to an opinion of Usher's that I mention not so much because of its novelty (for others have had the same idea) but because of the insistence with which he maintained it. This opinion, in its general form, was about the ability of inanimate[2] things or objects to begin to feel sensations. The idea was connected in his mind (as I have previously hinted) with the grey stones of the home of his ancestors.

The sensations arose, he imagined, from how these stones had been placed, one on top of the other, as well as from the fungi that spread over[3] them, and the decayed trees that stood around the building. And, he added, from the long period that the house and its reflection in the still waters of the lake had been left undisturbed.

The evidence of these sensations could be seen, he said, in how the water and walls had gradually created an atmosphere of their own. The result of this was evident, he added, in that terrible influence which for centuries had molded[4] the destinies of his family, and which made him what he was. Such opinions need no comment, and I will make none.

BELIEFS

- What does Usher believe about the things around him and about the house in which he lives? Tick.
  - ☐ He thinks the atmosphere of the house has had a good influence on his family.
  - ☐ He thinks the atmosphere of the house has had a bad influence on his family.

 The books we read, and which for years had occupied the mental existence of the invalid, were, as might be supposed, in strict keeping with Usher's beliefs.

We spent hours together studying works of the supernatural, demonism and the occult by authors such as Gresset, Macchiavelli, Swedenborg, Holberg, D'Indaginé, De la Chambre, Tieck, and Campanella. One favorite volume was an edition about the Inquisition, the *Directorium Inquisitorum*, by the monk Eymeric de Gironne, and there were passages in Pomponius Mela, about the old African Satyrs and OEgipans, creatures that were half man and half goat, over which Usher would sit dreaming for hours. His main delight, however, was found in the perusal of an exceedingly rare and curious book about a forgotten church, the *Vigiliae Mortuorum Secundum Chorum Ecclesiae Maguntinae*, which contained songs for the dead.

---

1 ballad [ˋbæləd] (n.) 敘事詩
2 inanimate [ɪnˋænəmɪt] (a.) 無生命的
3 spread over 蔓延
4 mold [mold] (v.) 形成
5 in strict keeping 息息相關
6 occult [əˋkʌlt] (n.) 神祕學

7 volume [ˋvɑljəm] (n.) 冊；書
8 edition [ɪˋdɪʃən] (n.) 版本
9 Inquisition [ˏɪnkwəˋzɪʃən] (n.) 宗教審判
10 passage [ˋpæsɪdʒ] (n.)（書中的）段；節
11 delight [dɪˋlaɪt] (n.) 愉快；樂趣
12 perusal [pəˋruzl̩] (n.) 細讀

- Do you read in your free time? What do you like to read?
- How much time do you spend reading every week?
- Where do you usually read? Work with a partner and compare your reading habits.
- What do Usher's reading habits tell us about him?

I could not help thinking of the probable influence that these books were having upon Usher, when, one evening, after informing me abruptly[1] that Lady Madeline was no more, he stated his intention of preserving[2] her corpse for a fortnight, before its final burial, in one of the numerous vaults[3] within the walls of the building. The reason for this unusual procedure[4] was one which I did not feel at liberty to dispute.

The brother had reached this decision, he told me, after considering the unusual nature of the malady of the deceased[5], and after considering that her doctors might interfere and ask questions about her illness, and because the family's burial ground was in a remote and exposed[6] place. I will not deny[7] that when I thought of the sinister[8] appearance of the physician who I saw on the day of my arrival at the house, I had no desire to oppose what I regarded as just a harmless, and by no means unnatural, precaution.

1 abruptly [əˈbrʌptlɪ] (adv.) 突然地
2 preserve [prɪˈzɝv] (v.) 保存
3 vault [vɔlt] (n.) 地窖的貯物室
4 procedure [prəˈsidʒɚ] (n.) 傳統 的做法
5 deceased [dɪˈsist] (n.) 死者
6 exposed [ɪkˈspozd] (a.) 無遮蔽的
7 deny [dɪˈnaɪ] (v.) 否認
8 sinister [ˈsɪnɪstɚ] (a.) 陰險的
9 arrangement [əˈrendʒmənt] (n.) 安排
10 entombment [ɪnˈtumənt] (n.) 下葬
11 coffin [ˈkɔfɪn] (n.) 棺材

At Usher's request, I personally helped him in the arrangements[9] for the temporary entombment[10]. The body was placed in a coffin[11], then we two alone carried it to its rest. The vault in which we placed the coffin had been closed for such a long time that our torches were half smothered[12] in its oppressive atmosphere and therefore we did not have an opportunity to investigate it.

The vault was small and damp[13], and did not admit any light. It lay at a great depth, immediately beneath my own bedroom. It had been used, apparently, in remote times, as a dungeon[14] and possibly as a torture chamber. It had then been used as a place for the deposit of gunpowder[15] or some other highly combustible[16] substance, since part of its floor and the whole interior of a long archway through which we had reached it, were carefully covered with copper. The door, of heavy iron, had also been similarly protected.

12 smothered [ˈsmʌðəd] (a.) 熄滅的
13 damp [dæmp] (a.) 潮濕的
14 dungeon [ˈdʌndʒən] (n.) 地窖
15 gunpowder [ˈgʌnˌpaudə] (n.) 火藥
16 combustible [kəmˈbʌstəbl̩] (a.) 可燃的

We placed Lady Madeline upon trestles[1] inside the vault, and then moved aside the unscrewed[2] lid of the coffin, and looked upon the face of the occupant[3]. My attention was now drawn[4] to the striking[5] similarity between the brother and sister, and Usher, probably guessing my thoughts, murmured a few words from which I learned that he and Lady Madeline had been twins.

Our stares[6] did not rest on the dead sister for long because we could not look at her without feeling disturbed. The disease which had caused Lady Madeline to die at this early age, had left, as was usual in all maladies that had trance-like symptoms, a faint blush[7] on her neck and face, and a lingering[8] smile on her lips. We replaced and screwed down the lid and, having locked the iron door, we made our way to the rooms in the upper part of the house.

THE BURIAL OF LADY MADELINE

- When someone dies, what is the normal reaction of that person's family and friends?
- How does Usher react when his sister dies?
- What is unusual about the burial of Lady Madeline?
- What do we find out about the 'malady' that killed her?
- What is the special connection between Usher and Lady Madeline?

1 trestle [ˋtrɛs!] (n.) 支架；台架
2 unscrewed [ʌnˋskrud] (a.) 螺絲未旋緊的
3 occupant [ˋɑkjəpənt] (n.) 佔有者
4 draw [drɔ] (v.) 吸引注意
5 striking [ˋstraɪkɪŋ] (a.) 驚人的
6 stare [stɛr] (n.) 凝視
7 blush [blʌʃ] (n.) 臉紅
8 lingering [ˋlɪŋgərɪŋ] (a.) 逗留不去的

After a few days of bitter[1] grief[2] had passed, there was a noticeable change in my friend's mental disorder. His usual manner had vanished[3]. His ordinary occupations were neglected[4] or forgotten. He moved from room to room. The paleness of his face had assumed[5] a more sickly color, and the light in his eyes had gone completely. His usual tone of voice was heard no more and instead he spoke with a trembling voice as if he were in great fear. There were times when I thought that his agitated mind was trying to keep some oppressive secret and that he was struggling for the courage to reveal it.

SECRETS

- Do you find it easy to keep a secret? Was there ever a time when you could not keep a secret?
- When is it right to tell a secret? When is it wrong to tell a secret?
- What do you think Usher's secret is?

At times I thought he was suffering from an inexplicable[6] form of madness, because I saw him gazing[7] vacantly for hours, as if listening to some imaginary sound. It was no wonder that his condition terrified me. I felt the wild influences of his fears creeping upon me, by slow yet certain degrees.

1 bitter [ˈbɪtɚ] (a.) 痛苦的
2 grief [grif] (n.) 悲痛
3 vanish [ˈvænɪʃ] (v.) 消失
4 neglect [nɪgˈlɛkt] (v.) 疏忽
5 assume [əˈsjum] (v.) 呈現
6 inexplicable [ɪnˈɛksplɪkəbl̩] (a.) 無法解釋的
7 gaze [gez] (v.) 凝視
8 retire [rɪˈtaɪr] (v.) 就寢
9 struggle [ˈstrʌgl̩] (v.) 努力
10 sway [swe] (v.) 搖擺
11 fitfully [ˈfɪtfəlɪ] (adv.) 斷斷續續地
12 to and fro 來回地
13 rustling [ˈrʌslɪŋ] (a.) 沙沙作響的

It was after retiring[8] to bed late on the night of the seventh or eighth day after we had placed Lady Madeline inside the vault, that I experienced the full power of this fear. I was unable to sleep and the hours slowly passed. I struggled[9] to understand the reason for these nervous feelings that had taken control of me. I tried to convince myself that much of what I felt was due to the influence of the gloomy furniture in the room, of the dark and tattered tapestries which, because of the storm outside, swayed[10] fitfully[11] to and fro[12] making rustling[13] noises about my bed.

But my efforts were useless. I could not stop myself from trembling, and my heart felt deeply alarmed. Shaking off my fear with a gasp[14] and a struggle, I sat up against my pillows. I stared into the intense darkness of the room, and listened to certain indistinct sounds which came at intervals through the pauses in the storm. I was overpowered[15] by an intense and unbearable[16] feeling of horror that I could not explain. I got dressed quickly (for I felt that I would sleep no more during that night), and tried to awake[17] myself from the condition into which I had fallen by walking rapidly around my room.

I had done this a few times when the sound of a light step on an adjoining[18] staircase caught my attention. I recognized it as Usher's footstep. An instant afterwards he knocked gently on my door, and entered, carrying a lamp. His face was, as usual, pale as a corpse, but in addition there was a kind of mad hilarity in his eyes. It was a kind of controlled hysteria[19]. His appearance upset me, but anything was preferable to the solitude that I had experienced. I even welcomed his presence as a relief.

---

14 gasp [gæsp] (n.) 喘氣
15 overpower [ˌovəˈpaʊɚ] (v.) 壓倒
16 unbearable [ʌnˈbɛrəbl̩] (a.) 不能忍受的
17 awake [əˈwek] (v.) 喚醒
18 adjoining [əˈdʒɔɪnɪŋ] (a.) 鄰接的
19 hysteria [hɪsˈtɪrɪə] (n.) 歇斯底里

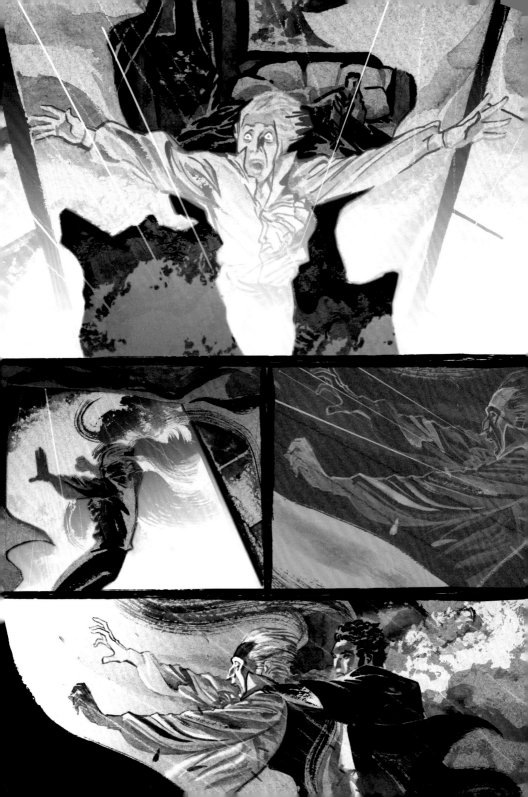

'And have you not seen it?' he said abruptly, after staring around him for some moments in silence. 'Have you not seen it? But, wait! You shall.' After carefully shading[1] his lamp, he hurried to one of the windows, and threw it open to the storm.

The sudden strength of the gust[2] of wind that entered nearly lifted us off our feet. It was a stormy night, but it was beautiful and terrible at the same time. A whirlwind[3] had apparently collected its force in our vicinity[4], for there were frequent, violent changes in the direction of the wind. The thickness of the clouds, which were so low that they were pressing upon the towers of the house, did not prevent us from seeing the speed with which they crashed against each other. We had no view of the moon or stars, and no lightning[5] flashes were visible. But the sky was glowing in the unnatural light of a clearly visible cloud of gas that hung about and covered the house.

'You must not – you shall not see this!' I said to Usher, as I led him, with a gentle violence, from the window to a seat. 'These sights, which confuse you, are just normal electrical phenomena, or perhaps they have their origin in the mist of the lake. Let us close this window. The air is cold and dangerous to your health. Here is one of your favorite romances[6]. I will read, and you shall listen, and in this way we will pass this terrible night together.'

---

1 shade [ʃed] (v.) 遮蔽
2 gust [gʌst] (n.) 一陣強風
3 whirlwind [ˋhwɝ‚lwɪnd] (n.) 旋風
4 vicinity [vəˋsɪnətɪ] (n.) 附近地區
5 lightning [ˋlaɪtnɪŋ] (n.) 雷電
6 romance [roˋmæns] (n.) 傳奇小說

The old book which I had picked up was the 'Mad Trist' by Sir Launcelot Canning. When I had called it a favorite of Usher's I meant it more as a sad joke than a serious comment. In truth, it is very long and boring and there is little in it that could be interesting for my friend. It was, however, the only book immediately at hand, and I hoped that the excitement that now agitated Usher might find relief in what I read. Judging by the intensity with which he listened, or appeared to listen, to the words of the story, I could congratulate myself on the success of my idea.

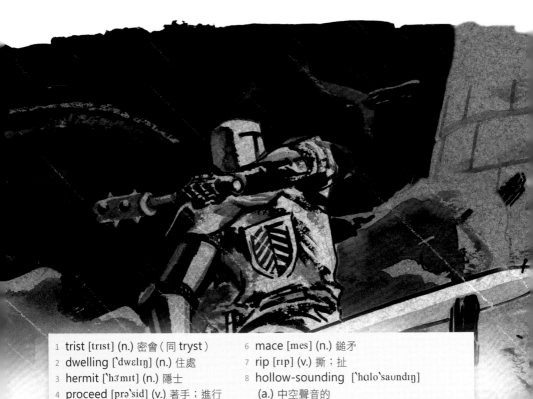

1 trist [trɪst] (n.) 密會 (同 tryst)
2 dwelling [ˋdwɛlɪŋ] (n.) 住處
3 hermit [ˋhɝmɪt] (n.) 隱士
4 proceed [prəˋsid] (v.) 著手；進行
5 spiteful [ˋspaɪtfəl] (a.) 懷恨的
6 mace [mes] (n.) 鎚矛
7 rip [rɪp] (v.) 撕；扯
8 hollow-sounding [ˋhɑloˋsaʊndɪŋ] (a.) 中空聲音的
9 reverberate [rɪˋvɝbə‚ret] (v.) 反響；迴盪

I had arrived at that well-known part of the story where Ethelred, the hero of the Trist, having tried in vain to enter the dwelling of the hermit peaceably, proceeds to enter it by force. The words of the story are as follows:

"And Ethelred, who was by nature a brave man, and who now felt very powerful thanks to the wine that he had drunk, did not wait any longer to speak to the hermit, who was an obstinate and spiteful man. Feeling the rain upon his shoulders, and fearing the coming storm, he lifted up his mace , and cracked and ripped the door, and tore everything apart, so that the noise of the dry and hollow-sounding wood alarmed and reverberated throughout the forest."

At the end of this sentence I started[1], and for a moment, paused; for it appeared to me – although I immediately decided that my excited imagination had deceived[2] me – that I had heard indistinctly, from some very remote part of the house, what might have been the echo (but a low and dull one certainly) of the same cracking and ripping sound which Sir Launcelot had described so exactly. It was, no doubt, the coincidence alone that had drawn my attention, because, in the middle of the rattling of the windows and the ordinary noises of the increasing storm, the sound in itself should not have disturbed me. I continued the story:

"But the good champion[3] Ethelred, now entering the door, was angry and amazed to see no sign of the hermit. Instead of the hermit he saw a huge scaly[4] dragon with a fiery[5] tongue, which sat on guard outside a palace of gold, with a floor of silver. A shield[6] of shining brass[7] hung on the wall, and on it these words were written:

Whoever enters here, is a conqueror[8]

Whoever kills the dragon, shall win the shield.

Ethelred lifted up his mace, and struck the head of the dragon, which fell before him and died with a cry so horrid and harsh [10], and so piercing [11], that Ethelred had to put his hands over his ears to protect them from the dreadful noise, the like of which he had never heard before." Again I paused abruptly. There could be no doubt that in this instance, I did actually hear – although it was impossible to say from where it came – a low and apparently distant, but harsh, long, and most unusual screaming or grating [12] sound – exactly as I had imagined the dragon's unnatural shriek [13] to be.

Although I was shocked by this second most extraordinary coincidence, and I felt confused by my feelings of wonder and extreme terror, I still kept sufficient presence of mind [14] to avoid alarming my nervous companion by making any observation. I was by no means [15] certain that he had noticed the sounds in question, although during the last few minutes a strange change had certainly taken place in his appearance.

He had gradually moved his chair, so that he was sitting facing the door of the room. I could only partly see his face, although I saw that his lips were trembling as if he were murmuring inaudibly [16]. His head had dropped down onto his chest, yet, from the wide and rigid opening of the eye as I caught a glance of it in profile [17], I knew that he was not asleep. The motion of his body, too, conflicted with this idea, because he rocked [18] from side to side with a gentle yet constant movement.

---

12 grating [ˈgretɪŋ] (a.) 刺耳的
13 shriek [ʃrik] (n.) 尖叫聲
14 presence of mind 鎮定；沉著
15 by no means 決不

16 inaudibly [ɪnˈɔdəblɪ] (adv.) 聽不見地
17 in profile 從側面地
18 rock [rɑk] (v.) 擺動

Having rapidly taken notice of all this, I resumed[1] the narrative of Sir Launcelot, which continued as follows:

"And now, the champion, having escaped from the terrible fury[2] of the dragon, thinking of the shield, and of breaking the enchantment[3] which was on it, removed the dragon's body from his path, and walked across the silver pavement[4] to where the shield was on the wall. It did not wait for his arrival, but fell down upon the silver floor at his feet, with a great and terrible ringing sound."

No sooner had these syllables passed my lips, than – as if at that moment a shield of brass had indeed fallen heavily onto a floor of silver – I became aware of a distant hollow metallic clanging sound, like a muffled[5] echo.

SENSES

- Do you think the narrator has really heard a sound or is it the power of suggestion?
- Have you ever thought you heard a sound when there was nothing there? What was the situation?

Completely unnerved[6], I leapt to my feet; but Usher's rocking movement was undisturbed. I rushed to the chair in which he sat. His eyes were fixed and staring, and his whole face was rigid. But, as I placed my hand upon his shoulder, his whole body shuddered[7]. A sickly smile trembled on his lips and I saw that he spoke in a low and hurried murmur, as if unconscious of my presence. Bending closely over him, I began to understand the horrible meaning of his words.

1 resume [rɪˋzjum] (v.) 重新開始
2 fury [ˋfjʊrɪ] (n.) 狂暴
3 enchantment [ɪnˋtʃæntmənt] (n.) 魔法
4 pavement [ˋpevmənt] (n.) 鋪過的路面
5 muffled [ˋmʌfḷd] (a.) 隱約的
6 unnerved [ʌnˋnɝvd] (a.) 失去勇氣的
7 shudder [ˋʃʌdɚ] (v.) 發抖；戰慄

'Not hear it? Yes, I hear it, and I have heard it. For many minutes, many hours, many days, I have heard it. Yet I did not dare. Oh, pity me, I am a miserable man! I did not dare. I did not dare to speak! We put her into the tomb while she was still living! Didn't I say that my senses were acute? Now I tell you that I heard her first weak movements in her coffin. I heard them many, many days ago, yet I did not dare to speak! And now tonight . . . the story of Ethelred! The breaking down of the hermit's door, the death-cry of the dragon, and the clanging of the shield! Instead there was the breaking open of her coffin, the grating of the iron hinges[1] of her prison, and her struggles inside the vault! Where can I run? Won't she be here soon? Isn't she hurrying to punish me for my haste[2]? I've heard her footsteps on the stairs. I can hear that heavy and horrible beating of her heart. Mad man!' He jumped to his feet, and screamed out this word, as if in the effort he were giving up his soul. 'Mad man! I tell you that now she is standing outside the door!'

As if his words had the power of a spell[3], at that moment the huge doors to which he pointed were thrown open. It was the force of the wind. But there, outside those doors, covered in a shroud[4], stood the tall figure of Lady Madeline of Usher. There was blood on her white robes[5], and the evidence of a struggle on every part of her emaciated[6] body. For a moment she remained there, trembling and moving slowly from side to side in the doorway. Then, with a low moaning[7] cry, she fell heavily onto her brother. And in her final violent dying moment, she brought him to the floor, dead. He was a victim[8] to those terrors that he had predicted[9].

44

1 hinge [hɪndʒ] (n.) 鉸鏈
2 haste [hest] (n.) 倉促
3 spell [spɛl] (n.) 咒語
4 shroud [ʃraʊd] (n.) 壽衣
5 robe [rob] (n.) 長袍
6 emaciated [ɪ`meʃɪ,etɪd] (a.) 極瘦的
7 moaning [`monɪŋ] (a.) 嗚咽的
8 victim [`vɪktɪm] (n.) 遇難者
9 predict [prɪ`dɪkt] (v.) 預言

I ran terrified from that room and from that house. The storm was still in full force as I crossed the old bridge. Suddenly a wild light shone along the path, and I turned to see where it could have come from since only the house and its shadows were behind me. The light was that of the full blood-red moon. It now shone vividly through that once barely visible crack that extended from the roof of the building to its base. As I watched, this crack widened rapidly. In shock I saw the great walls breaking apart. There was a long loud shouting sound like the voice of a thousand waters, and then the deep dark lake closed silently over the fragments of the 'House of Usher'.

AFTER READING

Ⓐ Personal Response

1 Now that you have read the story, can you say why it is called *The Fall of the House of Usher*?

2 Which part of the story was the most frightening, and why?

3 Would you like to visit the House of Usher? Explain why or why not?

4 What was unusual about the burial of Lady Madeline?

5 Which of the characters do you feel most sympathy for? Explain why.

6 In your opinion what mistakes did Roderick Usher make in his life? Is there anything he could have done to change the course of events? Make a list of suggestions.

B Comprehension

7 Tick (✓) T (True), F (False) or D (Doesn't say) below.

T F D	(a)	Was the narrator happy about visiting Roderick Usher?

| T F D | (b) | Was the narrator related to Usher? |

| T F D | (c) | Did Usher have any children? |

| T F D | (d) | Was Usher in good health? |

| T F D | (e) | Did the narrator speak to Lady Madeline during his visit? |

| T F D | (f) | Did the narrator think he could help Usher? |

| T F D | (g) | Did the doctor check that Lady Madeline was dead? |

| T F D | (h) | Was Usher sorry that his sister had died? |

| T F D | (i) | Was the narrator frightened by Usher's behavior during the storm? |

| T F D | (j) | Did Usher know that his sister was still alive? |

| T F D | (k) | Had Usher tried to murder his own sister? |

| T F D | (l) | Did Lady Madeline kill Usher? |

8 Match the words in Column A with the words of similar meaning in Column B.

A	B
mansion	burial
malady	stones
entombment	curtains
physician	house
draperies	sickness
masonry	doctor

9 Here are three summaries of the story. Which is the most accurate and why? Choose one summary and re-write it so that it is closer to the original story.

a) A man goes to stay with his friend Roderick Usher who lives alone with his valet in a large old house. Roderick is sick and disturbed. He is haunted by the ghost of his dead sister Madeline. One night during a fierce storm, Roderick goes completely mad, saying that Madeline was buried alive and that now she has come to take him away. He falls down dead from a heart-attack.

b) A man receives a letter from an old friend, Roderick Usher, inviting him to stay at his house and keep him company. The man hardly recognizes Roderick, who is not well physically or mentally. Roderick's sister Madeline dies and Roderick buries her in the vaults of the house. A week later there is a fierce storm. Madeline comes back to life and escapes from her coffin. She finds her brother and kills him.

c) A man visits his old friend Roderick Usher. Both Roderick and his sister Madeline are sick. The man keeps Roderick company and tries to cheer him up, but Madeline dies while he is staying at the house. He helps Roderick bury her body. During a storm, Madeline appears in the house after escaping from her coffin. In reality she had been asleep and Roderick had buried her alive. Madeline collapses dead on top of her brother and he dies instantly.

10 Talk about a place where you have had to stay. Describe:

a) Why you were there.
b) What your room was like.
c) The sensations you had going into the place and if you would like to live there.

C Characters

11 Work with a partner. What facts do you know about the narrator, Roderick, and Madeline? Write two sentences about each of these characters.

12 Here is an extract from a police report describing Roderick Usher. See if you can complete it using information from the story.

People who knew Roderick Usher said that he had

changed a lot in recent years. They say that his skin was

as _____ as that of a _____. His eyes

had become _____ and _____. In fact

people found the _____ of his skin and the

_____ look of his eyes quite startling. His lips

were said to be _____ and very _____.

He had a _____ nose, but his _____ were

broad. His _____ was finely-shaped and he had

a _____ forehead. His hair could be described as

_____ and _____ like a web, but it was

also very _____ and _____. Judging by

his appearance he did not seem at all _____.

13 Do you think that Roderick Usher is mad? Look for evidence in the story to support your theory. Make a list of any behavior that seems normal or abnormal to you.

14 At the beginning of the story we learn that Roderick Usher has written a letter to his friend asking him to come and stay at the House of Usher. Use the information from the story to write Usher's letter of invitation.

Begin like this

> My dear friend,
>
> It has been many years since our last meeting . . .

End the letter like this

> I look forward to your response.
>
> Your most affectionate friend,
>
> Roderick

15 'Lady Madeline's disease had puzzled her doctors for a long time'. What were her symptoms and what was their probable cause? Imagine you are her doctor. Write a report about the state of her health. Give your advice for her recovery.

> The causes of Lady Madeline's illness are not entirely clear . . .

16 Choose one of the characters in the story - Roderick Usher, Lady Madeline or the narrator. Write a sequence of entries from this character's diary, explaining the events of the story from his/her point of view. Work individually or with a partner.

❶ Plot and Theme

17 Put these events from the story in the correct order.

_1_   ⓐ Arriving at the House of Usher the narrator discovers that his friend Roderick Usher is sick.

_____   ⓑ There is a storm and the narrator cannot sleep.

_____   ⓒ Usher and the narrator bury Lady Madeline in a coffin in the house's vaults.

_____   ⓓ Lady Madeline appears in the doorway.

_____   ⓔ The narrator learns that Usher's sister Madeline has a strange disease.

_____   ⓕ Usher and the narrator pass the time reading and painting.

_____   ⓖ The narrator escapes but the house falls apart and breaks into fragments.

_____   ⓗ Usher and the narrator hear screams.

_____   ⓘ Lady Madeline dies and falls on Usher, killing him.

_____   ⓙ The narrator tries to calm Usher by reading to him.

_____   ⓚ Usher tells the narrator that Lady Madeline is dead.

18 What is the main theme of the book? In groups read and discuss the list of possible themes below. Are any of these the theme of *The Fall of the House of Usher*? If not, write your own summary of the theme.

ⓐ Forces that we do not understand control our destiny.

ⓑ Sooner or later people pay for the wrong-doings of their ancestors.

ⓒ Objects are like living things and have a life of their own.

ⓓ Isolation from the world brings death.

ⓔ What we believe will happen, does really happen.

19 Some of the objects and events in *The Fall of the House of Usher* have a symbolic meaning. Can you match the items on the left with the ideas on the right?

a The crumbling state of the house

b The lake that reflects the house

c The storm

d The house's empty windows

e The bridge outside the house

1 The emptiness of life in the House of Usher

2 A link with the outside world

3 Usher's image as reflected in his twin sister

4 The decaying state of the Usher family

5 Usher's madness

20 Have you noticed any other parts of the story that may have a symbolic meaning?

21 What part does the weather play in the story? Imagine you are reporting on the storm in the story. Describe it in a short weather report for the local newspaper. Use some of the notes:

Freak Storm Causes Chaos

A freak storm hit the region late last night.

A whirlwind _____.

Storm was _____.

Clouds _____.

It was not possible to see _____.

The light _____.

The moon _____.

The walls of the House of Usher _____.

TEST

1 Listen to a detective questioning the narrator about events at the House of Usher. Then tick (✓) the correct statements.

_____ 1 a There was a crack in the back wall of the house.

 b There was a crack in the front wall of the house.

_____ 2 a He could only listen to piano music.

 b He couldn't listen to anything other than stringed instruments.

_____ 3 a Madeline was entombed in the family grave yard.

 b Roderick entombed Madeline in an old dungeon.

_____ 4 a The narrator heard Lady Madeline escaping from the vault.

 b The narrator didn't hear Lady Madeline escaping from the vault.

2 Read the questions and tick (✓) the correct answers.

_____ a When the narrator arrived at the House of Usher, he found his friend Roderick incoherent. Why was he incoherent?

 1 He was very nervous.

 2 He was drunk.

 3 He had been drugged.

 4 He was emotional.

_____ b Roderick had a terrible fear. What was it?

 1 a fear of water

 2 a fear of danger

 3 a fear of death

 4 a fear of disease

54

_____ [c] What was the narrator impressed by?
   1. Roderick's paintings
   2. Roderick's guitar playing
   3. Roderick's song lyrics
   4. Roderick's dancing

_____ [d] How did the narrator feel when Roderick came to his room on his last night at the House of Usher?
   1. terrified
   2. relieved not to be alone any more
   3. miserable
   4. angry

3 Get into pairs. Student A look at the picture on page 21. What relevance does it have to the story? What can you see in the picture? Tell Student B.

Student B look at the picture on page 45. What relevance does it have to the story? What can you see in the picture? Tell Student A.

4 You have just read *The Fall of the House of Usher*. Write a book report describing the story.

   1. Say what kind of story it is.
   2. Describe the setting and characters.
   3. Summarize the plot.
   4. Give opinions on the story and characters.
   5. Would you recommend the story to a friend?

5 Read the text below and choose the most suitable word for each space.

Roderick's (a) .... sister, Madeline was seriously ill when Roderick's friend arrived at the House of Usher. Roderick was very upset because Madeline was his only (b) .... relative and he was afraid she would die. Doctors (c) .... by her illness. Her body was wasting away and she (d) .... fell into a deep sleep.

One evening, Roderick told his friend that his sister (e) .... He wanted to keep his dead sister in a coffin in a vault for two weeks and then bury her in the family's burial ground.

However, Madeline wasn't dead and seven or eight days later, in the (f) .... of a terrible storm, she escaped from her tomb and climbed the stairs to the room (g) .... Roderick and his friend sat. For a moment, the pale emaciated woman stood in the doorway and then she died, (h) .... her brother and killing him.

a	① twin	② older	③ younger	④ half
b	① livelier	② lively	③ life	④ living
c	① are puzzled	② puzzled	③ were puzzled	④ have puzzled
d	① never	② frequently	③ almost	④ fairly
e	① had died	② died	③ dead	④ is dying
f	① duration	② time	③ middle	④ end
g	① that	② which	③ where	④ when
h	① fell on	② falling on	③ fall on	④ had fallen on

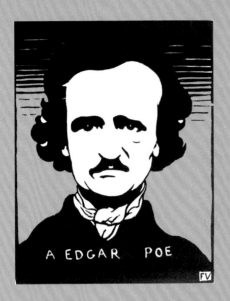

A EDGAR POE

THE OVAL PORTRAIT

ABOUT THE BOOK

The Oval Portrait was first published in 1842 as *Life in Death*. Poe subsequently[1] edited[2] and cut the story and it was republished as *The Oval Portrait* three years later. It is one of Poe's shortest stories but includes themes that recur through many of his works such as death and monomania[3] (a type of paranoia[4] where the sufferer is obsessed with a single idea or emotion). Elements from the story inspired Oscar Wilde's novel, The Portrait of Dorian Gray.

The Oval Portrait is a story within a story. It starts with an injured narrator taking refuge[5] for the night in an abandoned mansion in the mountains. He is drawn to the paintings in the room where he is sleeping and finds a book that describes them. One painting in particular strikes[6] him and when he reads about it in the book his interest is explained.

The story focuses on the relationship between art and life. In the story art and life are rivals. An extreme obsession[7] with art can lead to death, as art takes the vital forces from life in the creative process.

Extreme obsession (monomania) is recurrent[8] in many of Poe's tales. In *The Fall of the House of Usher* Roderick Usher is ruined by his own fear. In *The Masque of the Red Death* Prince Prospero's obsession with the disease, the Red Death, ultimately leads to his own death.

---

1 subsequently [ˈsʌbsɪˌkwɛntlɪ] (adv.) 隨後
2 edit [ˈɛdɪt] (v.) 編輯
3 monomania [ˌmɑnəˈmenɪə] (n.) 偏執狂
4 paranoia [ˌpærəˈnɔɪə] (n.) 偏執狂；妄想狂
5 refuge [ˈrɛfjudʒ] (n.) 庇護
6 strike [straɪk] (v.) 觸動
7 obsession [əbˈsɛʃən] (n.) 執迷
8 recurrent [rɪˈkɜənt] (a.) 週期性的

1 Look at these pictures from the story. Write six
questions about them. Exchange questions with your
partner. Then, write answers to your partner's questions.
Keep these answers in a safe place.

2 What do you think *The Oval Portrait* will be about?
Tick (✓) below.

- a A man who meets the woman of his dreams
- b The story of an old house
- c A man who is afraid of the dark
- d An unhappy love story
- e The story of someone who appears in a painting
- f A ghost story

3 Listen to the start of the story. Tick (✓) T (True) or F (False).

T F a The narrator is called Pedro.
T F b The narrator is hurt.
T F c They do not have the owner's permission to enter
        the house.
T F d No one had lived in the house for a long time.
T F e The room they went to was very austere.
T F f The narrator was struck by the paintings.

4 Imagine that you have to stay alone in an old house. Describe what it looks like. You decide to sleep in one of the house's bedrooms. Describe the room. Tell your story to the other students in your group. Whose story was the best?

5 Here are some words that appear in the story. Match them to their definitions.

a	abandoned	1	hated the thought of
b	surrounded	2	left empty, not repaired, and not taken care of
c	gazed	3	fooled or cheated
d	entranced	4	were all around
e	dreaded	5	hypnotized; fascinated
f	deceived	6	looked for a period of time

6 Use the words above to complete these sentences.

a The house seemed to have been _____ quite recently.

b The only things she _____ were the tools that stole her lover from her.

c I wanted to make sure that my sight had not _____ me.

d I asked Pedro to open the black velvet curtains that _____ the bed.

e For a very long time I read, and I _____ at the paintings.

f For one moment, the painter stood _____ before his work.

7 Take a look at the woman in the painting. Think about the following questions. Then imagine you are the woman and write a short presentation of yourself. (Approximately 3 minutes). Give the presentation in class.

- ⓐ Who do you think she is?
- ⓑ What is her name?
- ⓒ How old is she?
- ⓓ Where does she live?
- ⓔ What are her likes and dislikes?
- ⓕ In what period is she living?
- ⓖ Why is she the subject of the painting?

8 Match the following genres to the paintings below. Choose one of the genres and use the Internet to find out as much about it as possible. Write a report.

_____ ⓐ Pop Art
_____ ⓑ Still Life
_____ ⓒ Landscape
_____ ⓓ Portrait

9 Now as you read the story, note the answers to these questions:

- ⓐ Where does the story take place?
- ⓑ What did the narrator find on his pillow?
- ⓒ Where did the painter work?

10 Make up another three questions to ask your partner, after they have finished reading.

fter my accident, my servant Pedro broke into¹ an
empty house so that I would have a place to shelter
and would not have to spend the night in the open air. We
were in the Apennine mountains and the house we had
found was both grand and gloomy. It seemed to have been
abandoned quite recently.

We made ourselves comfortable in one of the smallest
rooms that was not as sumptuously² furnished as the others.
It lay in a remote tower of the building.

Its decorations were rich, yet tattered³ and old. Tapestries⁴
and weapons covered the walls, together with a very large
number of lively modern paintings in rich gold frames.
These paintings hung on all the main walls of the house but
also in its many corners. I was slightly delirious⁵ and this is
probably why the paintings drew my attention.

THE ACCIDENT

- Have you ever had an accident or been ill while you were
  away from home? What happened?
- What kind of accident do you think the narrator had?

1 break into 闖入
2 sumptuously [ˈsʌmptʃuəslɪ] (adv.) 奢華地
3 tattered [ˈtætɚd] (a.) 破爛的
4 tapestry [ˈtæpɪstrɪ] (n.) 掛氈
5 delirious [dɪˈlɪrɪəs] (a.) 譫妄的

Since it was already night, I asked Pedro to close the heavy shutters[1] of the room, to light the candles, and to open the black velvet curtains that surrounded the bed. I wanted all this to be done so that even if I couldn't sleep, I could at least look at these pictures and read through the small volume that I had found on my pillow, which discussed and described them in detail.

For a very long time I read, and I gazed[2] at the paintings. The hours passed and midnight came. I did not like the position of the candelabrum[3], but rather than disturb my sleeping servant, I stretched out my hand with difficulty and moved it so that it threw its rays more fully on the book that I was reading.

This action produced an effect that I had not expected. The rays of the numerous candles now fell on a corner of the room that had previously been in the shadow. Because of this I saw in vivid[4] light a picture that I had not noticed before. It was the portrait of a young girl who was just ripening[5] into womanhood. I glanced[6] at the painting, and then closed my eyes. I was not sure why I did this. It was an impulsive movement and I wanted to make sure that my sight had not deceived me. In a few moments I looked again fixedly[7] at the painting.

---

1 shutters [ˈʃʌtəz] (n.)〔複〕百葉窗
2 gaze [gez] (v.) 凝視
3 candelabrum [ˌkændəˈlɑbrəm] (n.) 燈臺
4 vivid [ˈvɪvɪd] (a.) 生動的
5 ripen [ˈraɪpən] (v.) 變成熟
6 glance [glæns] (v.) 瞥見
7 fixedly [ˈfɪksɪdlɪ] (adv.) 固定地
8 vignette [vɪˈnjɛt] (n.) 暈映畫（背景逐漸暗淡的畫像）

Now I was wide awake and sure of what I had seen. The portrait, I have already said, was that of a young girl. It was a painting of her head and shoulders, done in what is technically termed a 'vignette' manner. The arms, the chest, and even the ends of her radiant hair melted into the deep shadow that formed the background of the whole picture. The painting's frame was oval, richly gilded⁹ and very ornate¹⁰. As a work of art nothing could be more admirable than the painting itself, but it was not the skill of the painting or the immortal beauty of the face that had made such an impression on me. Nor had I mistaken the head for that of a living person.

Thinking earnestly¹¹ upon these points. I remained, for an hour perhaps, half sitting, half reclining¹², with my eyes fixed on the portrait. Eventually, I felt I understood the true secret of its effect and I fell back into the bed.

---

9 gild [gɪld] (v.) 裝飾
10 ornate [ɔrˋnet] (a.) 裝飾華麗的
11 earnestly [ˋɝnɪstlɪ] (adv.) 認真地
12 recline [rɪˋklaɪn] (n.) 躺

I had found that the spell of the picture was due to the expression on the face, which was so lifelike and alive. At first I found it shocking, then it confused me and then finally it horrified me.

With a sense of deep and reverent[1] admiration I returned the candelabrum to its former position. Now that the cause of my agitation[2] was out of sight, I looked for the volume that discussed the paintings and their histories. Turning to the description that identified the oval portrait, I read the following:

"She was a young woman of great beauty and full of joy. It was an evil time when she saw, loved, and married the painter. He was passionate[3], studious, and austere[4], and he was already married to his love of painting. She was beautiful and full of joy, all light and smiles. She loved all things, hating only the art of painting, which was her rival. The only things she dreaded were the pallet[5] and the brushes and the other tools that stole her lover from her. For this reason it was a terrible thing for this lady to hear the painter say that he wanted to paint her.

But she was obedient, and she sat meekly[6] for many weeks in the dark room of a high tower, where the light fell from above onto the pale canvas[7] of the painting. The painter loved his work, which continued from hour to hour, and from day to day. He was a wild and moody[8] man, who became so lost in his dreams that he did not see that the health and spirits of his bride were affected. She pined[9] visibly to all but him.

PORTRAITS

- Do you like having your photograph taken?
- Would you like to have your portrait painted?
- Why did the young bride not want to have her portrait painted?

1 reverent [ˋrɛvərənt] (a.) 恭敬的
2 agitation [ˌædʒəˋteʃən] (n.) 激動
3 passionate [ˋpæʃənɪt] (a.) 熱烈的
4 austere [ɔˋstɪr] (a.) 嚴厲的；刻苦的
5 pallet [ˋpælɪt] (n.) 調色板

6 meekly [ˋmiklɪ] (adv.) 溫順地
7 canvas [ˋkænvəs] (n.) 油畫布
8 moody [ˋmudɪ] (a.) 喜怒無常的
9 pine [paɪn] (v.) 憔悴

Yet his bride smiled on and on without complaining because she could see that the painter (who was well-known) took such pleasure in his work. He worked day and night to paint the woman who loved him so much. Yet she grew weaker and more dispirited every day.

Some people who saw the portrait spoke in low voices of how marvelous it was, and how it was proof of the painter's deep love for her. As his work came to an end, the painter admitted[1] no one into the tower.

He had grown wild with passion for his work, and he rarely looked away from the canvas even to look at the face of his wife. He did not see that the tints[2] that he spread on the canvas were taken from the cheeks of the woman who sat beside him.

Many weeks had passed, and very little remained to do, except for one brushstroke on the mouth and one tint on the eye. The brush was applied, and then the tint was placed.

For one moment, the painter stood entranced[3] before his work, but the next moment, while he was still staring at the painting, he started to tremble with terror and turned very white.

He cried out in a loud voice, 'This is indeed life itself!' Then he turned suddenly to look at his beloved: she was dead!

OBSESSIONS

- Do you think that people can become obsessed with their work, their studies or their hobbies?
- Can you think of any examples? Has this ever happened to you?

---

1 admit [əd'mɪt] (v.) 准許進入   3 entranced ['ɛntrənst] (a.) 狂喜的
2 tint [tɪnt] (n.) 色彩

AFTER READING

Ⓐ Personal Response

1 How much of the story of *The Oval Portrait* did you guess just by looking at the pictures? Look at the answers that you wrote to your partner's questions before reading the story. Compare them with what you have just read.

2 Look again at *Before Reading Exercise 2* (page 59). Which statement correctly summarizes what the story is about? Give reasons for your answer.

3 The narrator sheltered in the house because he had had an accident. Can you guess what might have happened to him? Have you ever hurt yourself in an accident? Where were you? What happened? Who helped you? Work in a group. Tell the other students about your experience.

4 Do you feel sorry for the young woman in the portrait? Why? Why not? What advice would you have given her? Write her a short letter. Begin like this:

> My dear friend,
>
> I am very worried about you.
> If you take my advice, you should . . .

5 Discuss the following questions and give reasons for your answers:

  (a) Is this a good story?
  (b) Does any part of it frighten you?
  (c) What would you do to improve the story?
  (d) Can you think of a different ending?

ⓑ Comprehension

6 Read these statements about *The Oval Portrait* and tick (✓) T (True), F (False) or D (Doesn't say) below. Discuss your answers with the students in your group. Do you all have the same answers?

T F D a The narrator and Pedro chose to stay in the largest room in the house.

T F D b The narrator learned about the painting from a description in a book.

T F D c The young woman and her husband were very similar in character.

T F D d When the painter was working on the portrait, people visited the house.

T F D e The young woman was afraid of her husband.

T F D f The painter painted his wife's portrait because he loved her.

7 Study the sentences below that are taken from the text. Find these sentences in the story, and then explain what the underlined words refer to.

a It lay in a remote tower of the building.

b I was not sure why I did this.

c At first I found it shocking, then it confused me and then finally it horrified me.

d "This is indeed life itself!"

8 Explain the following questions to a partner using your own words.

a Why did the narrator find the painting shocking?
b Why did the young woman dread the painter's pallet and brushes?
c Why did the painter not notice that his young wife was ill?
d Why did the painter tremble when he saw the finished painting?

9 Join the pairs of sentences below to make one sentence containing a defining or non-defining relative clause. Look at the examples below.

The main tools were the pallet and the brushes. The painter used them.
↪The main tools that the painter used were the pallet and the brushes.

The painting took a long time to complete. It was perfect.
↪The painting, which took a long time to complete, was perfect.

a Pedro was the narrator's servant. He broke into the empty house.
↪ _____

b The house was abandoned. It was the painter's old house.
↪ _____

c The narrator read the book. He had found it on his pillow.
↪ _____

d The painter was lost in his dreams. He was a moody man.
↪ _____

e The people saw the portrait. They said it looked like the painter's wife.
↪ _____

f The young woman became weak and depressed. She was once full of energy.
↪ _____

C Characters

10 Write the words and phrases under the correct person or object.

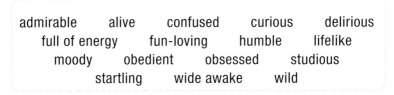

admirable   alive   confused   curious   delirious
full of energy   fun-loving   humble   lifelike
moody   obedient   obsessed   studious
startling   wide awake   wild

The Narrator   The Painter   The Painter's Wife   The Painting

11 Imagine you are the narrator and that you have access to the Internet. Write an e-mail home saying that you had an accident, explaining how it happened and how you feel.

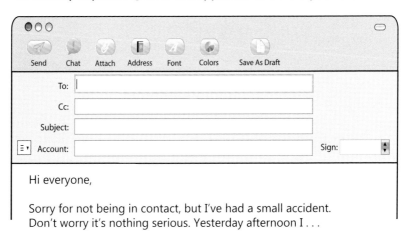

Send   Chat   Attach   Address   Font   Colors   Save As Draft

To:

Cc:

Subject:

Account: Sign:

Hi everyone,

Sorry for not being in contact, but I've had a small accident. Don't worry it's nothing serious. Yesterday afternoon I . . .

12 We are told that the painter 'had become obsessed with his work'. What does he do that shows his obsession?

13 Who in the story might have said the following words?

- a 'Go away! You can't come in here any more!'
- b 'This is so lifelike!'
- c 'Please, don't worry about me, I am fine.'
- d 'Pedro, could you close the shutters of the room?'
- e 'I have to paint you.'
- f 'He must be deeply in love with his wife.'

14 Rewrite the sentences above in reported speech. Use these verbs:

exclaim   insist   refuse   ask   declare   persuade

Example

'Go away! You can't come in here any more!'
↪ *The painter refused to let his visitors come in any more.*

15 Work with a partner and invent the rest of the conversations around each quote. Role-play them in class.

16 Imagine you are the painter. Explain what happened. Defend yourself by explaining what happened from your point of view.

ⓓ Plot and Theme

17 *The Oval Portrait* is really a 'story within a story'. Do you agree? If so, what titles would you give to:

ⓐ The story _____

ⓑ The story within the story _____

18 Put the following sentences in the correct order:

1   ⓐ The narrator and his servant made themselves comfortable in an abandoned house.

_____ ⓑ He looked up the description of this oval portrait in the book and read it.

_____ ⓒ The painter did not allow anyone to enter the place where he was working.

_____ ⓓ When he finally finished his painting, he discovered that his wife was dead.

_____ ⓔ His wife's health was affected, but he did not notice.

_____ ⓕ At one point, he noticed a very lifelike portrait in the corner of the room.

_____ ⓖ A beautiful young woman married a painter, but he was obsessed with his work.

_____ ⓗ As he worked on her portrait day after day, she became weak and depressed.

_____ ⓘ The paintings on the walls of the house fascinated the narrator.

_____ ⓙ On his pillow he found a book that contained descriptions of these paintings.

_____ ⓚ One day the painter decided to paint a portrait of his bride.

19 Which of the following do you most agree with? Put them in order of importance to you.

1   a) Art is more important than life because it lasts forever.

_____ b) Art is different from life and we should not confuse the two.

_____ c) We should value life more than art.

_____ d) Life is imperfect, but art is always perfect.

_____ e) Art is in competition with life, and since art is better, it always wins.

_____ f) Art is important because it lives on after death.

_____ g) When art copies life, it steals something from life.

_____ h) The painter was right to love his painting more than his wife.

_____ i) The painter's wife died because she was too beautiful.

_____ j) Art helps us to remember the beauty of the past.

20 Find an English language newspaper and study some of the headlines. Can you guess the content of the stories they relate to? Read *The Oval Portrait* headlines below. What do you think they refer to?

a) ARTIST ACCUSED OF WIFE'S DEATH

b) POLICE ARREST APENNINE HOUSE BURGLARS

c) Painter kidnapped our daughter, claim bride's family

d) INJURED MAN FOUND SAFE

21 Can you invent some similar headlines of your own?

22 Choose one of the newspaper headlines above and, working with a partner, write a short article related to the events of the story.

TEST

1 Can you remember the story? Read the following
sentences first. Then listen to the conversation and check
your answers.

- a) The portrait hung in an (1) _____ house in the
  Apennine (2) _____.
- b) The narrator of the story was with his (3) _____,
  Pedro when he saw the portrait.
- c) Large (4) _____ hung on all the main walls of the
  gloomy old house.
- d) The portrait fascinated the narrator because it was very
  (5) _____.
- e) The narrator learnt all about the portrait from a little
  book on his (6) _____.

2 Now listen to the conversation and check your answers.

3 The *Mona Lisa* is a famous portrait. Write an entry
about the *Mona Lisa* for the little book that the narrator
of the story found. You can use the Internet to help you.
Think of the following questions.

- a) Who was Mona Lisa?
- b) Who painted her?
- c) What is special about the portrait?
- d) Where is it now?
- e) What do you think of the *Mona Lisa*?

4 Read the statements below about the story. Tick (✓) T (True) or F (False).

   T F   ⓐ The oval portrait of the girl had a simple gold frame.

   T F   ⓑ The portrait made an impression on the narrator because it was very skillfully painted.

   T F   ⓒ The narrator was not sure why he was so drawn to the painting.

   T F   ⓓ The narrator was shocked by the lifelike quality of the portrait.

   T F   ⓔ The girl shared her husband's passion for art.

   T F   ⓕ The girl was very happy when her husband said that he wanted to paint her.

5 Work in pairs. Student A look at Portrait A. What can you see in the picture? What does the picture tell you about the woman? What style is used to portray the woman? Imagine you are the woman, introduce yourself to Student B and tell each other about yourselves.

Student B look at Portrait B. What can you see in the picture? What does the picture tell you about the woman? What style is used to portray the woman? How are the pictures different?

A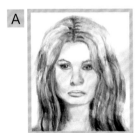
B

6 Read the questions and tick (✓) the most suitable answer to each one.

_____ ⓐ Who noticed that the painter's wife was growing weaker and weaker?

- ① nobody
- ② everybody but the painter
- ③ her family
- ④ his family

_____ ⓑ Why didn't the girl complain?

- ① She was happy so she said nothing.
- ② She enjoyed being painted.
- ③ Her husband never listened to her complaints.
- ④ She loved her husband and she knew he really enjoyed painting.

_____ ⓒ What happened to the girl's cheeks as the artist painted her?

- ① They grew redder and healthier.
- ② They disappeared.
- ③ They grew paler and lost their color.
- ④ They grew brighter and she looked happier.

_____ ⓓ What did the painter realize in the end?

- ① The painting was terrible.
- ② The painting was in fact real. It had sucked the life out of his wife.
- ③ The painting didn't look like his wife.
- ④ The painting wasn't as beautiful as his wife.

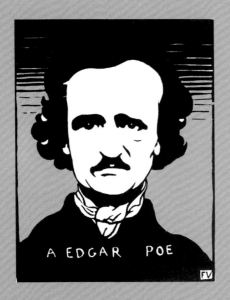

A EDGAR POE

FV

THE MASQUE OF THE RED DEATH

ABOUT THE BOOK

The Masque of the Red Death was first published in 1842 and it is an allegorical[1] tale about the inevitability of death. The story uses many features of Gothic fiction such as physical and psychological fear, castles, feudal[2] society and death.

The story is set in an unnamed time and place. A terrible disease, the Red Death, is spreading[3] rapidly throughout the land, killing everyone it meets. Prince Prospero, along with one thousand noble friends, escapes to an isolated abbey where he is sure they will be happy and safe.

After several months he organizes a fancy-dress ball[4] in a set of rooms that have been decorated in different colors. The last room is decorated in black and has a black clock that rings every hour. However on the stroke of midnight[5] an uninvited guest arrives, dressed as the Red Death.

The story is a very good example of Poe's Gothic horror short stories. Poe creates a dark and uneasy atmosphere and the story focuses on images of blood and death, while the personification of the Red Death adds an element of the supernatural. *The Masque of the Red Death* also reflects Poe's vision of what a short story should be like. According to Poe, a short story should be so well written that every word, from beginning to end, contributes to the overall effect. In this story a series of powerful symbolic images and an impeccable[6] narrative voice are tightly woven[7] into a macabre[8] tale of horror with great insight into the human condition.

---

1 allegorical [ˌæləˈɡɔrɪkl] (a.) 寓言的
2 feudal [ˈfjudl] (a.) 封建的
3 spread [sprɛd] (v.) 蔓延
4 fancy-dress ball 化妝舞會
5 stroke of midnight 半夜十二點整
6 impeccable [ɪmˈpɛkəbl] (a.) 無懈可擊的
7 weave [wiv] (v.) 交織
8 macabre [məˈkɑbə] (a.) 令人毛骨悚然的

BEFORE READING

1 Work with a partner. Look at these illustrations from the book for two minutes. Close the book, and write down all the words and phrases associated with the illustrations that you can think of.

2 Choose one of the illustrations and, using your words, describe what is happening in the picture. Add and invent details if you wish.

3 Give your story to a partner and get them to continue it, predicting what is going to happen next. Share your stories with the rest of the class.

4 Look quickly through the illustrations in the book. Do they have anything in common? What atmosphere do they suggest? What elements in the illustrations contribute to the atmosphere (subject, color, light, style, etc.)?

🎧 36 **5** Listen to Prince Prospero and then answer the questions below.

    ⓐ Who is he speaking to?

    ⓑ What is happening in the country?

    ⓒ Where does he want to go?

    ⓓ What supplies does he take with him?

🗣 **6** Based on the listening, choose two adjectives from the list below that describe Prince Prospero. Tell a partner why you think they are the most suitable.

    ⓐ careful

    ⓑ charitable

    ⓒ generous

    ⓓ foolish

    ⓔ frightened

    ⓕ fun

    ⓖ imprudent

    ⓗ optimistic

7 Prince Prospero organizes a 'masked ball' for his friends. Imagine that you are planning a party. Prepare a checklist of all the things that you have to do. Now design an invitation to your party.

8 Colors have symbolic meaning in the story. What do you associate with the following colors? You can choose from the list below or add your own ideas.

white　　　BROWN　　　GRey　　　Red

GReeN　　ORANge　　　Blue　　Black

balance	death	hope	money	power
blood	dirt	jealousy	mystery	purity
boredom	elegance	life	nature	sadness
creativity	energy	love	passion	tradition
danger	happiness	luck	peace	warmth

9 Close your eyes and think of a person or thing that you associate with each color. Write a sentence about each one.

10 What do you think the *Red Death* of the story's title refers to? Perhaps you have already guessed. Talk to your partner and find out if you have the same answer. Now read the first two sentences of the story to find out if you were correct.

For a long time the 'Red Death' had devastated the country. No pestilence[1] had ever been so fatal, or so terrible. It started and ended in the blood – in the redness and the horror of blood. There were sharp pains, and sudden dizziness, and then heavy bleeding from the pores[2] of the skin, and then death.

Red marks upon the body and especially on the face of the victim were sure signs of the disease. The whole attack, progress and termination of the disease lasted half an hour.

But Prince Prospero was happy and fearless and wise. When his territories were half empty, he called into his presence a thousand healthy and cheerful friends from among the knights and ladies of his court, and with these he retired to the isolation[3] of one of his fortified[4] abbeys[5]. This was an extensive and magnificent place, the creation of the prince's own eccentric[6] yet grand taste.

THE RED DEATH

- Why is this disease called the Red Death?
- What do you think might have caused it?
- What is the best way to control or cure diseases like this?
- What infectious diseases exist today and how are we dealing with them?

1 pestilence [ˈpɛstləns] (n.) 瘟疫
2 pore [por] (n.) 毛孔
3 isolation [ˌaɪsl'eʃən] (n.) 孤立
4 fortified [ˈfɔrtə,faɪd] (a.) 加強防禦的
5 abbey [ˈæbɪ] (n.) 大修道院
6 eccentric [ɪkˈsɛntrɪk] (a.) 古怪的

A strong, high wall circled it. This wall had iron gates. The servants, using furnaces[1] and hammers, welded[2] the bolts[3] of the gates. They intended to leave no means of entry or exit if inside there were sudden signs of despair or panic[4]. The abbey had plenty of supplies[5]. By taking these precautions the courtiers defended themselves against the possibility of infection. The external world could take care of itself.

In the meantime it was foolish to feel sorry, or to think. The prince had provided everything that would give pleasure. There were fools, there were entertainers, there were ballet dancers, there were musicians, there was beauty, there was wine. All this, and security, were inside. Outside was the 'Red Death'.

It was towards the close of the fifth or sixth month of his isolation, while outside the pestilence was at its worst, that Prince Prospero entertained[6] his thousand friends at a splendid masked ball[7].

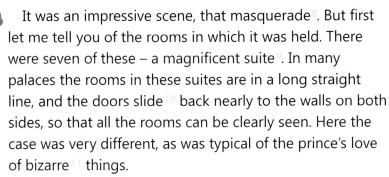

PRINCE PROSPERO

- What kind of person is Prince Prospero?
- Do you agree that he is 'happy and fearless and wise'?
- Does his name have any special significance?
- Where would you choose to be – inside the abbey with Prince Prospero or outside risking the danger of infection by the 'Red Death'?

It was an impressive scene, that masquerade[8]. But first let me tell you of the rooms in which it was held. There were seven of these – a magnificent suite[9]. In many palaces the rooms in these suites are in a long straight line, and the doors slide[10] back nearly to the walls on both sides, so that all the rooms can be clearly seen. Here the case was very different, as was typical of the prince's love of bizarre[11] things.

The rooms were built in such an irregular way that it was only possible to see one room at a time. There was a sharp[12] turn every twenty or thirty yards[13], and at each turn there was a new effect.

---

1 furnace ['fɝnɪs] (n.) 熔爐
2 weld [wɛld] (v.) 熔接
3 bolt [bolt] (n.) 門栓
4 panic ['pænɪk] (n.) 恐慌
5 supplies [sə'plaɪs] (n.) 在此指食物和水
6 entertain [ˌɛntə'ten] (v.) 款待
7 masked ball 化妝舞會
8 masquerade [ˌmæskə'red] (n.) 化妝舞會
9 suite [swit] (n.) 組合
10 slide [slaɪd] (v.) 滑
11 bizarre [bɪ'zɑr] (a.) 奇異的
12 sharp [ʃɑrp] (a.) 急轉的
13 yard [jɑrd] (n.) 碼

To the right and the left, in the middle of each wall, a tall, narrow Gothic[1] window looked onto a closed corridor that followed the twists and turns of the suite. These windows were of stained glass[2]. Their color matched the decorations of the room into which they opened. The room at the eastern extremity, for example, was decorated in blue – and its windows were vividly blue.

The second room had purple ornaments and tapestries[3], and here the glass in the windows was purple. The third room was green, and so were the windows. The fourth was furnished and lit with orange – the fifth with white – the sixth with violet. The seventh apartment was covered in black velvet tapestries that hung all over the ceiling and down the walls, falling in heavy folds on a carpet of the same material and color. But in this room only, the color of the windows was not the same as the decorations. The window panes[4] here were scarlet, a deep blood color.

NUMBERS AND COLORS

- What is your lucky number? What is your favorite color?
- What is the significance of numbers and colors in the story? Work with a partner and compare your ideas. Then, search the Internet for further information about the meaning of numbers and colors.

There were no lamps or candle holders in any of the seven rooms. There was no light of any kind from lamps or candles inside the rooms. But in the corridors that followed the suite, a heavy tripod, carrying a brazier[5] of fire, stood opposite each window. The rays of the fire illuminated the room brightly through the tinted glass, and this produced a multitude of colorful and fantastic effects.

But in the western or black room the effect of the fire's light shining through the blood-tinted panes on to the dark tapestries, was ghastly[6] in the extreme. And it produced such a wild look on the faces of those who entered, that very few of the company were courageous enough to set foot inside it.

In this room there also stood against the western wall a gigantic clock made of ebony[7]. Its pendulum[8] swung back and forward with a dull, heavy, monotonous clang[9]. When the minute hand had circled the clock's face, and the hour struck, a clear, loud, deep and exceedingly musical sound came from the clock. It was such a strange sound that, at the end of each hour, the musicians of the orchestra had to pause, momentarily, in their performance, to listen to the sound. Because of this the dancers had to stop their evolutions[10], and the enjoyment of the whole company was interrupted.

1 Gothic [ˈgɑθɪk] (a.) 哥德式建築的
2 stained glass 彩繪玻璃
3 tapestry [ˈtæpɪstrɪ] (n.) 掛氈
4 pane [pen] (n.) 窗玻璃片
5 brazier [ˈbreʒɚ] (n.) 火盆
6 ghastly [ˈgæstlɪ] (a.) 恐怖的
7 ebony [ˈɛbənɪ] (n.) 黑檀木
8 pendulum [ˈpɛndʒələm] (n.) 鐘擺
9 clang [klæŋ] (n.) 鏗鏘聲
10 evolution [ˌɛvəˈluʃən] (n.) 進展

While the chimes[1] of the clock were still ringing, the most energetic dancers grew pale, and the older and more sedate[2] ones seemed confused or thoughtful. But when the echoes of the chimes had stopped, laughter immediately spread through the group.

The musicians looked at each other and smiled as if they were smiling at their own nervousness and foolishness. And they whispered to each other that the next time the clock chimed it would not affect them again in the same way. Then, after a lapse[3] of sixty minutes, (just three thousand, six hundred seconds later) the clock chimed once more and there were the same feelings of concern, agitation and wonder[4] as before.

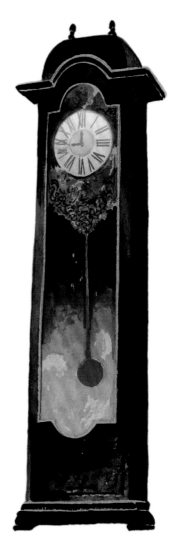

> **TIME**
>
> - Do you wear a watch? How often do you check it?
> - How important is time in your life? How does time play a role in the story?
> - How is time represented? What is Edgar Allen Poe telling us about the subject of time?

In spite of these things, it was a cheerful and magnificent party. The tastes of the prince were strange. He had a fine eye for colors and effects. His plans were bold, and his ideas were wild. Some people might have thought he was mad. His followers felt that he was not.

For this party he had organized the decoration of the seven rooms himself, and he had also suggested how the guests should dress. They had a grotesque[5] appearance.

There was much glare[6] and glitter[7] and energy and fantasy. There were strangely dressed figures and odd costumes that seemed the work of a madman. Much was beautiful, wild, bizarre, and terrible, and there was also much that might have produced feelings of disgust.

---

1 chimes [tʃaɪmz] (n.) 〔作複數形〕樂鐘聲
2 sedate [sɪˋdet] (a.) 沉著的
3 lapse [læps] (n.) 流逝
4 wonder [ˋwʌndɚ] (n.) 驚異
5 grotesque [groˋtɛsk] (a.) 怪誕的
6 glare [glɛr] (n.) 引人注目
7 glitter [ˋglɪtɚ] (n.) 燦爛奪目

Dancing through the seven rooms to the wild music of the orchestra, there was a multitude of fantastic characters, colored by the light from the windows. And then the ebony clock, standing in the black velvet hall, struck. For a moment everything was still and silent except for the voice of the clock. The dancers seemed to freeze. But when the echoes of the chime died away there was laughter. After the music returned, the dream-like figures continued dancing back and forth[1] more merrily than ever. But none of the dancers entered the seventh room.

The night was fading and a red light flowed through the room's blood-colored panes, and the blackness of the sable[2] tapestries became more terrifying. Those who stepped on the sable carpet heard a chime from the ebony clock that was more solemn[3] than any sound heard by those who were enjoying themselves in the other rooms.

---

1 back and forth 來來回回地
2 sable [ˈsebḷ] (a.) 黑色的
3 solemn [ˈsɑləm] (a.) 嚴肅的

THE MASKED BALL

- Have you ever been to a fancy-dress party? Who or what did you go as? What was your costume like?
- If you were going to a fancy-dress party now, what kind of costume would you like to wear?

   The other apartments were densely crowded, and the heart of life beat in them feverishly[1]. The party went on, until soon the clock began to strike midnight. Then the music and the dancers and all other things stopped as before. But now twelve strokes[2] had to be sounded by the clock, and this gave the more thoughtful guests time to think.

Before the last echoes of the last chime, many individuals in the crowd had noticed the presence of a masked figure that no one had seen before. The rumor of this new presence spread around in whispers. There was a murmur of disapproval from the whole company. Then this turned into a murmur of terror, of horror, and of disgust.

In an assembly of people like the ones I have described, someone of ordinary appearance would not have caused such feelings. Anything and everything was allowed that night, but the figure in question³ had gone beyond even the prince's limits. There are chords⁴ in the hearts of even the most badly behaved people that cannot be touched without causing emotion. There are some things about which it is impossible to joke.

---

1 feverishly [ˈfivərɪʃlɪ] (adv.) 狂熱地   3 in question 討論中的
2 stroke [strok] (n.) 時鐘響聲   4 chord [kɔrd] (n.) 弦

The whole company seemed now to feel that the costume and the behavior of the stranger had no humor or good taste at all. The figure was tall and thin, and was shrouded[1] from head to foot in the clothes of the grave. The mask that hid the face resembled the face of a stiffened[2] corpse[3] so closely that it would have been difficult to tell the difference between the mask and a real face. While the guests did not approve of this, they might have tolerated it, but this actor had gone so far as to assume the appearance of the Red Death. His clothes were covered in blood – and his broad forehead and all the features of his face were sprinkled[4] with the scarlet horror.

When Prince Prospero saw this spectral[5] figure walking among the dancers with a slow and solemn movement, at first he trembled either from terror or distaste[6] but then his face reddened with rage.

'Who dares', he demanded hoarsely[7] of the servants who stood near him. 'Who dares insult us with this blasphemous[8] mockery[9]? Stop him and unmask him, so that we may know whom we have to hang[10] at sunrise from the tower!'

---

1 shroud [ʃraʊd] (v.) 裹以屍衣
2 stiffened [ˈstɪfn̩d] (a.) 僵硬的
3 corpse [kɔrps] (n.) 屍體
4 sprinkle [ˈsprɪŋkl̩] (v.) 灑
5 spectral [ˈspɛktrəl] (a.) 幽靈的
6 distaste [dɪsˈtest] (n.) 憎厭；嫌惡
7 hoarsely [ˈhorslɪ] (adv.) 嗓音嘶啞地
8 blasphemous [ˈblæsfɪməs] (a.) 褻瀆的
9 mockery [ˈmɑkərɪ] (n.) 嘲弄
10 hang [hæŋ] (v.) 吊死

THE STRANGER

- Who is the stranger? What is strange about his behavior? What do you think he wants?
- Why are the guests horrified by his appearance?
- Why does he make Prince Prospero so angry?

Prince Prospero stood in the eastern or blue room as he spoke these words. They rang throughout the seven rooms loudly and clearly, for the prince was a bold, robust man, and the music had become hushed[1] at the waving of his hand.

The prince was standing in the blue room with a group of pale-faced servants by his side. At first, as he spoke, this group rushed in the direction of the intruder[2], who at that moment was close by and who, with a deliberate step, moved closer to the prince. But everyone was so shocked by the actor that no one tried to stop him, and he moved close to the prince without being stopped.

---

1 hush [hʌʃ] (v.) 使安靜
2 intruder [`ɪntrudɚ] (n.) 入侵者

The great assembly, as if with one thought, moved back from the centers of the rooms to the walls. With the same solemn and measured[1] step which had distinguished him from the beginning, the figure made his way without interruption through the blue room into the purple, through the purple into the green, through the green into the orange, through this again into the white, and then into the violet room.

It was then, however, that Prince Prospero, mad with rage[2] and the shame of his own momentary cowardice[3], rushed through the six rooms. No one followed him because of the terror that they all felt. The prince carried a dagger[4] and had approached rapidly to within three or four feet[5] of the figure, when the latter[6], having reached the velvet room, turned suddenly and faced his pursuer[7]. There was a sharp cry – and the dagger dropped onto the sable carpet, upon which, instantly afterwards, Prince Prospero fell down dead.

1 measured ['mɛʒəd] (a.) 平穩的
2 rage [redʒ] (n.) 狂怒
3 cowardice ['kauədɪs] (n.) 膽小；懦弱
4 dagger ['dægə] (n.) 短劍
5 foot [fut] (n.) 呎
6 the latter 指前文最後所提者
7 pursuer [pə'suə] (n.) 追捕者

Summoning the wild courage of despair, a group of the guests ran into the black room and tried to stop the actor, whose tall figure stood motionless in the shadow of the ebony clock.

They gasped in horror when they found that the shroud and the corpse-like mask were not inhabited by any tangible form.

And now the presence of the Red Death was acknowledged. He had come like a thief in the night. And in the bloodstained halls of their celebration, one by one the partygoers dropped and died. And the life of the ebony clock went out with that of the last of the merry-makers. And the flames of the tripods went out, and darkness and decay and the Red Death held dominion over all.

8 summon [ˋsʌmən] (v.) 召喚
9 motionless [ˋmoʃənləs] (a.) 一動不動的
10 gasp [gæsp] (v.) 喘息
11 shroud [ʃraʊd] (n.) 屍衣；壽衣
12 tangible [ˋtændʒəbl] (a.) 可觸知的
13 dominion [dəˋmɪnjən] (n.) 統治

Ⓐ The Three Stories

🗨 **1** Look at these three illustrations from the stories you have just read. In groups discuss the following questions.

- ⓐ Which stories do they belong to?
- ⓑ Are they representative of the stories?
- ⓒ What are the similarities in the illustrations?
- ⓓ What are the differences?
- ⓔ Design a new cover for the book.

🗨 **2** Compare the three main characters of all three stories. What are the similarities? What are the differences? Discuss in pairs.

Roderick Usher   The Painter   Prince Prospero

3 What is the effect of the narrator in each story? Does he reflect the author's point of view? Is the narrator neutral or does he affect our interpretation of the story? Is the narrator reliable in these stories? Give reasons for your answers.

❸ Personal Response

🗨 **4** Work with a partner. What did you like the most about the story and what did you dislike the most?

🗨 **5** Did this story remind you of any other stories you have read or films you have seen? Tell the rest of the class about them.

6 In which country do you think the story takes place? Give reasons for your answer.

7 When do you think the story takes place? Look for examples in the story to support your answer.

8 'He had come like a thief in the night.' Who is the author referring to? What does the author mean?

9 Is there anything in the story that you would have liked to change? Can you think of any way to improve the story?

C Comprehension

10 Answer the following questions.

  a In the story, why was the disease called the 'Red Death'?
  b Why did the servants weld the bolts of the gates?
  c When was the disease at its worst?
  d How many friends did the prince take with him to the abbey?
  e What color was the fourth room?
  f How were the guests dressed?
  g Which room were the guests afraid of and why?
  h What happened when the clock chimed?
  i At what time did the stranger appear?
  j What was the prince going to do to the stranger?
  k How did the prince die?
  l What happened to the guests at the ball?

11 Look again at the pictures illustrating this story. Write a short caption for each picture of one sentence or less.

12 In groups compare your captions. Choose one from each group for each picture.

13 Prince Prospero designed a suite of rooms. Which of the following colors did he use to decorate the rooms?

black	grey	red
blue	orange	violet
brown	pink	white
green	purple	yellow

14 Put these sentences from the story in the right order:

_1_   [a] The whole attack, progress and termination of the disease lasted half an hour.

_____   [b] It was an impressive scene, that masquerade.

_____   [c] And the life of the ebony clock went out with that of the last of the merry-makers.

_____   [d] There was no light of any kind from lamps or candles inside the rooms.

_____   [e] The rumor of this new presence spread around in whispers.

_____   [f] The prince was standing in the blue room with a group of pale-faced servants by his side.

_____   [g] But when the echoes of the chimes had stopped, laughter immediately spread through the group.

_____   [h] The prince had provided everything that would give pleasure.

15 Find words in the story that match the meanings below:

[a] A type of party   [d] A sound made by a clock

[b] A set of rooms   [e] The glass in a window

[c] A kind of knife   [f] People who play in an orchestra

16 Use your imagination to complete this invitation to Prince Prospero's party. Include the following information:

[a] Time
[b] Date
[c] Place
[d] Dress code
[e] Entertainment

Prince Prospero has great pleasure in inviting you to a . . .

Ⓓ Characters

17 Imagine you are a reporter who is going to interview Prince Prospero, the narrator and the uninvited stranger. Prepare three questions for each of them. Next, work with two or three other students. Read your questions out to the group.

18 Work with a partner to write up your interview with one of the story's three characters. Act out your interview to the rest of the class.

19 Who is the 'actor' who appears at the Prince's party? Describe him. Why are the partygoers horrified by him?

20 How does Prince Prospero's reaction to the events in his country reveal his character?

21 Does Poe approve of Prince Prospero and his actions? Discuss in pairs.

22 Prince Prospero is writing a journal. Some of his words have faded from the parchment. Use words from the story to complete his entry.

We have now been here in the _____ for about

_____ or _____ months. We have plenty of

_____ and tomorrow I will _____ my friends

to a _____ ball. I will, of course, hold this in the

_____ of _____ rooms that I have personally

designed. The _____ are built in an _____ way

and each one is decorated in a different _____ .

My favorite room is the black room, which is on the

_____ side. Its color is _____ and its walls are

covered in velvet _____ of the same color. The

windows here are a deep _____ color. The effect

this creates is _____ in the extreme. I'm sure

no one will be _____ enough to set _____ inside

this room. I think I'm going to have a lot of fun.

23 Work with a partner to write another entry from Prince Prospero's journal. Read this entry to the class.

❸ Plot and Theme

24 Work with two or three other students and discuss the following statements. Are any of these the message of the story?

    ⓐ Life is short so enjoy it while you can.
    ⓑ You can escape many things but not death.
    ⓒ We cannot help everyone so we must look after ourselves.
    ⓓ In difficult times, we should always be positive.

25 What do you think is the significance of the following:

    ⓐ The seven rooms? Think about what other things come in groups of seven.
    ⓑ The gigantic ebony clock? Think about how the clock is described.
    ⓒ The prince's name? What do you think it means?
    ⓓ The words 'masque', 'mask' and 'masquerade'? Use your dictionary to help you understand these words.

26 If you have read *The Fall of the House of Usher,* did you notice any similarities between that story and this one? Can you match the events from *The Fall of the House of Usher* with the following phrases from *The Masque of the Red Death*?

    ① '. . . the prince's love of bizarre things . . . '
    ② '. . . he called into his presence a thousand healthy and cheerful friends . . . '
    ③ 'No pestilence had ever been so fatal, or so terrible.'
    ④ 'This wall had iron gates. The servants, using furnaces and hammers, welded the bolts of the gates.'
    ⑤ '. . . instantly afterwards, Prince Prospero fell down dead . . . '

_____ a Lady Madeline was suffering from a disease that her doctors could not cure.

_____ b Roderick Usher had a strange collection of books.

c Usher and his sister fall down dead on the ground.

_____ d Usher and the narrator seal the lid of Lady Madeline's coffin and lock the vault's iron door.

_____ e Usher invites the narrator to stay at his house and keep him company.

27 Work with your partner and try to find examples of links between the two stories. Share these with the rest of the class.

28 Poe's Red Death resembles a real disease that was present in Europe in the Middle Ages: the Bubonic Plague or Black Death. What contagious diseases are still a problem in today's world? What is being done to stop them?

29 Childhood illnesses and infections are rapidly disappearing in many countries due to advances in medicine and inoculation campaigns. What illnesses of this kind do you know about, and have you ever suffered from one? How long did it last and what were the symptoms? What helped you recover?

1 Read the description of Prince Prospero and choose the most suitable word for each space.

A terrible plague was devastating the country and half the population had (a) _____ died. Prince Prospero, (b) _____ was a wise man, decided to escape to the safety of an isolated abbey with a thousand of his healthy friends. He locked (c) _____ and his friends into the abbey and he locked the world and the plague out. He left his people to their terrible fate.

After five or six months of isolation, the Prince decided to entertain his friends with a magnificent masked ball. The ball (d) _____ in a suite of seven rooms and each room was decorated in a different color. The seventh room was decorated in black and it had blood red windows, which cast ghastly shadows (e) _____ the room and the guests. Not many people had the courage to enter this room.

When the clock struck midnight, some of the guests noticed a masked figure that they (f) _____ before. To the horror and disgust of the assembled guests, the masked figure had dressed (g) _____ a victim of the Red Death.

At first Prince Prospero was afraid but then his fear turned to anger. Who dares to mock us? He cried. He shall be hung (h) _____ dawn. The masked corpse moved towards the prince and the guests moved back. The masked figure moved slowly towards the black room and the Prince followed. When he reached the black room, he turned and faced the Prince. Prince Prospero let out a cry and fell down dead.

[a]	① almost	② already	③ yet	④ although
[b]	① who	② that	③ whose	④ which
[c]	① herself	② his own	③ him	④ himself
[d]	① was holding	② were held	③ was held	④ held
[e]	① across	② under	③ behind	④ out of
[f]	① didn't see	② hadn't seen	③ haven't seen	④ weren't seen
[g]	① as	② of	③ for	④ from
[h]	① for	② in	③ on	④ at

2 Imagine that you were the only guest at the masked ball to survive. Write a letter to a friend in another country and tell him/her all about the ball.

    [a] What did you wear?
    [b] How were the rooms decorated?
    [c] How did you feel about the black room?
    [d] Did you go in there?
    [e] What happened at the ball?
    [f] How did you escape?
    [g] Do you approve of what Prince Prospero did?

3 With a partner look at the picture on page 97. Ask and answer questions about it.

> How do the people in the picture feel?

> They are very frightened.

4 Read the questions and tick (✓) the most suitable answers.

_____ ⓐ How could you tell that someone had the Red Death?

  ① The victims had a red mark on their noses.
  ② They had red marks on their bodies and on their faces.
  ③ They had red marks on their feet.
  ④ Their bodies were red.

_____ ⓑ What did Prince Prospero and his friends eat inside the abbey?

  ① Food was brought to them daily.
  ② They ate in restaurants in the neighborhood.
  ③ They didn't eat.
  ④ They ate the supplies already inside the abbey.

_____ ⓒ The seven rooms, in which the masked ball were held, were arranged so that . . .

  ① all the rooms could be clearly seen.
  ② you could only see the room you were in.
  ③ you could see into the next room.
  ④ you could see into each of the seven rooms.

____ d Why did the musicians stop playing when the gigantic ebony clock struck the hour?

1 They were tired and needed a break every hour.

2 They liked the sound that the clock made.

3 The guests wanted to know what time it was.

4 They were very strongly affected by the chimes of the clock.

____ e When did the guests start to notice the figure dressed as the Red Death?

1 After the death of Prince Prospero.

2 When the clock chimed at midnight.

3 When one of the guests screamed.

4 When Prince Prospero told them to unmask the terrible figure.

作者簡介 愛倫坡於 1809 年 1 月 19 日出生在美國麻薩諸塞州的波士頓，才兩歲時父母便雙亡，由蘇格蘭商人約翰‧愛倫撫養長大。

愛倫坡分別在英、美兩國接受教育，是個極為優秀的學生，並因而進入維吉尼亞大學和著名的西點軍校就讀。後來愛倫坡在部隊裡待了兩年，也就是在這段期間，他完成了前兩本詩集，並分別在 1827 年及 1829 年出版。

愛倫坡曾替若干家報章雜誌擔任過新聞記者和評論家的工作，此外，還寫了許多則短篇故事，包括《莫格街凶殺案》（1841 年出版）、《陷阱與鐘擺》（1843 年出版），和《黑貓》（1843 年出版）。這些故事所講述的，都是些深沉、陰暗又令人不安的主題，在美國，愛倫坡曾由於他那種「哥德式」的寫作風格而飽受批評，不過在歐洲，他的作品卻頗受歡迎，而且影響又深遠。

愛倫坡曾飽受疾病和憂鬱症之苦，而一些親密家人的過世更讓他備受打擊，其中包括深愛著他的年輕妻子維吉妮亞。為了減緩憂鬱的症狀，他縱情於杯中物，而過度的酗酒又讓他健康出狀況。愛倫坡的筆桿生涯沒讓他賺到什麼錢，因此生活十分潦倒，甚至債台高築，最後於 1849 年 10 月 7 日與世長辭。

愛倫坡對世界文壇的主要貢獻，即是促成短篇故事發展成一種正式的藝術形式。

本書簡介 本書所收錄的三則故事《艾家大院的崩塌》、《橢圓形肖像》和《紅死病的面具》，正是依循所謂「哥德式」傳統的短篇故事之絕佳範例。哥德式文學是在十八世紀末席捲英國，探索人性和人生經驗中的黑暗面，如死亡、惡魔、疏離、憂鬱、瘋狂和荒涼寂寞的環境等。把歌德式文學帶到美國的正是愛倫坡，而他在每一篇故事中所創造出的氛圍，不是屬於肉體層面的不安和戰慄，便是精神層面的憂慮和恐怖，至於這些故事中所一再出現的主旋律，則是瘋狂和死亡。

其中《艾家大院的崩塌》是 1839 年付梓的，也是他最受歡迎的恐怖故事之一，內容涵蓋了哥德式故事所有必要的特色：一棟讓人渾身發毛的建築、一幅與世隔絕的景色、一場神祕的疾病、狂風暴雨的天候，以及陷於困擾中的人物等等。這是一篇講述精神錯亂的羅德瑞‧艾舍，與他那位怪異的雙胞胎妹妹瑪德蓮之間的故事，如今已被公認為古典短篇故事中的超完美傑作。

愛倫坡在這篇故事中創造出一種所謂「幽閉恐懼症」的感覺，書中人物無法在屋內自由自在地走動，而且要直到房屋真正的崩塌，故事的敘述者才得以逃離。瑪德蓮和羅德瑞是雙胞胎，而這也分別阻礙了他們發展成完整的個體，還有，瑪德蓮雖然被埋，但她仍活著，並且在最後襲擊她哥哥，把他給壓死。

這篇故事也給了許多其他作品不少靈感，包括電影、歌劇、戲劇、流行音樂、電玩，以及無以數計的小說創作。

1 艾家大院的崩塌

P.13

那天已經入秋，整日裡陰霾不開，四野俱寂，半空中雲層低懸。我騎著馬，踽踽獨行於一大片分外淒涼的荒野，最後在暮色降臨時，終於見到了那座陰鬱的艾家大院。當我一見到這棟建築時，一股難以忍受的哀戚便襲遍全身。

　　我望著眼前的這片景象，目光也不時盯在那座大宅院本身。只見周遭一大片的單調景觀，一面面蕭瑟的牆壁，一扇扇有如空洞雙眼的窗戶，雜亂的芒草，以及幾株枯木所殘留下來的白色樹幹。我的心情一時之間也隨之盪到谷底，那種鬱悶的感覺就像是過足了鴉片癮之後，從如夢似幻中乍然醒過來一般。頓時之間一股刺骨的寒意襲遍全身，一顆心感到寒冷而沉重。到底是什麼東西在作祟，讓我一想到艾家大院，就會如此莫名地驚惶失措起來？這是個無解的謎團，縱然費盡心機的推敲，也無法應付那些紛至沓來的迷離幻影。

地方

• 你是否造訪過一處這樣的地方，在一見到它時，就立刻有股快樂或是哀傷的氣氛猛然襲來？請描述一下當時的感受，為什麼這處地方會讓你有如此的感覺？

• 和當時的天氣有關嗎？還是和那兒的地貌或是人們有關？

P.14

無奈之餘，我只好強迫自己為此下了個不怎麼讓人滿意的結論：這世界的確有些東西是超乎我們理解範圍的，而眼前的這幅景象要是拿來重新安排一下的話，或許就不致於讓我留下這麼哀戚鬱悶的印象了。就在這麼想的當兒，胯下的坐騎已來到一處黑濛濛的小湖邊，艾家大院就矗立湖畔。我俯視湖面，只見那些灰茫茫的芒草、有如鬼魅般蒼白枯幹、如空洞雙眼的房間窗戶，在湖光的倒映之下顯得更加扭曲猙獰。

然而，我還是打定主意，要在這棟幽暗迷濛的大宅院裡待上幾個星期。屋主羅德瑞・艾舍是我童年時代的死黨，在闊別多年後，我最近收到了他的來信，信中顯示他在精神上受到了極大的困擾。他在信中提到，除了在肉體上飽受疾病的折磨外，思緒更是一片混亂和恍惚，此外，他也提到我是他最好的朋友，更是唯一的知交，要是有我的相伴，一定可以減輕他的痛苦。展信讀後，我便立刻答應了他的要求，沒有片刻猶豫。

115

羅德瑞・艾舍

- 故事的敘述者是如何認識羅德瑞・艾舍的？
- 艾舍為什麼要寫信給這位敘事者？
- 艾舍要求這位敘事者做些什麼？

P.15

雖然打從孩提時代，我們便過從甚密，但是我對這位老友卻所知有限。他為人矜持而內斂，不過就我所知，多年來他的家族在許多藝術創作中，都顯現出不凡的才氣，還不遺餘力的從事各種慈善活動，對於音樂也是忘情地投入。不過，我更知道一件事：他們的家族沒分支旁系，也就是說，整個家族都是一脈單傳，而且一直都是如此，沒什麼太大的變化。

P.16

我開始在想，這座大宅院的特性與居住在裡面的那些人的個性，簡直可以稱得上「絕配」，而且我又猜想，在漫長的幾個世紀以來，這兩者之間極可能彼此影響著。看來情況的確是如此，由於缺乏旁系後裔，再加上家族名字和宅院名字均是在父傳子的一脈單傳下，最後終於讓這兩個名字合而為一，而

形成這筆產業的名稱「艾家大院」。當地的鄉里村民都這麼稱呼，「艾家大院」等於是這個家族和家族莊園的代名詞。

家族

- 我們對艾家大院到底有哪些了解？請在正確的答案上打勾：
  - ☐ 羅德瑞有個枝繁葉茂的大家族。
  - ☐ 羅德瑞的家族對藝術極有興趣。
  - ☐ 羅德瑞的家族是在最近才繼承了這座莊園。
  - ☐ 艾家大院始終都是小小的。
- 現在再想想你自己的家族，你可以追溯自己的家譜到多遠？

P.17

當我抬起目光，把視線由莊園在湖中的倒影再度移向莊園本身時，一股奇怪的想法不由得在心中油然而生。這個想法簡直荒謬得可以，我之所以一提，只是想表達那股壓迫我身上的情緒反應是多麼地強烈。我一直全神貫注於自己的想像中，以致於到後來真的開始相信：由整座莊園周遭與附近地區所產生的氛圍，似乎和天上的空氣無關，而是從腐朽的枯木、灰牆，以及一片死寂的小湖所散發出來的，那兒充斥了神祕難測的瘴癘之氣。

抖落掉這些夢境似的情緒，我仔細地端詳起這座大宅院。宅院的主要結構看來飽經風霜，外表的色澤早已褪盡，細小的青苔爬滿了整面外牆，偌大的一片蜘蛛網從簷角邊垂掛下來，但磚塊仍保持良好的狀態，石塊也只有零星的破損，這和剛才的景象之間存在著某種極

不協調的感覺。撇開這種腐朽破敗的跡象不談，整棟建築的結構看不出來是危樓，只是眼尖的人或許可以看出來，在沿著前面的屋頂而下，有一道甚難查覺的裂縫正順著牆面蜿蜒曲折地消失在湖水中。

注意到這種種情況後，轉眼間我已策馬騎過一座小橋，來到了大宅院裡。有個僕人順手牽走我的馬，我走進一座有著哥德式拱門的大廳，另一個侍童一言不發地領著我穿過幾條黑壓壓又蜿蜒曲折的走廊，最後來到主人的房間。我一路上所看到的絕大部分東西，都加深了先前所提過的那些感覺。周遭的物品、天花板上的雕刻、牆上懸著的黝黑掛氈、烏漆抹黑的地板，以及一走過便會咯吱作響的盔甲，這些都是自幼以來便刻劃在心中的記憶。

P.19

不過我仍然覺得很驚訝，面對這些尋常景象在我身上所激起的幻想，那種感覺竟如此生疏。在跨出其中一道樓梯時，突然巧遇到艾家的家庭醫師，我發現他的臉上似乎掛著一種十分困惑的表情。只見他有些焦躁地走過我旁邊，然後那位侍童便推開一扇門，陪同我來到主人的面前。

我發現自己置身在一個寬敞高聳的房間裡，窗戶長而窄，而且和黑色的木質地板相距甚遠，使得即使站在屋內，雙手也搆不到窗戶。只見燈光微弱地透過窗框流瀉到屋內，把周遭一些顯眼的東西照得更清晰些，不過，要想瞧清楚屋內遠一點的角落或是天花板的話，則

顯得吃力。黑色的帷幕一條條地從牆上垂落下來，傢俱也是一付老態龍鍾的樣子，甚至破破爛爛的，許多書本和樂器零亂地四處散落著。頓時之間我彷彿覺得呼吸到一股哀傷的氣氛，而且陰鬱的氣息也似乎滲透到每一樣東西裡面。

具有警示意味的跡象

• 想想看敘事者到目前為止所看見的以及所想的。那兒到底有什麼跡象會提醒我們：艾家大院的確有些地方不對勁？

P.20

當我一走進去，原本躺在沙發上的艾舍一骨碌地站了起來，熱情相迎。我起初覺得他太多禮了，反而顯得有些矯情，不過再瞧瞧他的那張臉，卻不由得相信這完全是出於一片真心誠意。

我們入座之後，有好長一段時間都默不作聲。我半是憐憫、半是恐懼地盯著他猛瞧。說真格的，決沒有一個人會像羅德瑞•艾舍一樣，竟在這麼短暫的時間裡產生如此驚人的變化，因此讓我難以認出眼前這個面色有如白蠟的傢伙，就是我的兒時玩伴。

不過他臉上的輪廓還是很突出，雖然膚色憔悴蒼白得有如死屍，但一雙大眼睛卻十分清澈，閃爍著逼人的光

芒，雙唇單薄、缺少血色，但嘴唇的弧線仍然優雅。他鼻子的輪廓頗為細緻，但鼻孔卻很大。他的下巴很挺，髮絲則如蜘蛛絲一般纖柔。把這種種特色湊在一起，再配上那寬闊的前額，讓他的容貌令人難以忘記。到了現在，這些特色又似乎更誇張了些，而且有關於他的每一樣東西又是那麼地與眾不同，我不由得懷疑眼前和我說話的這個人，難道真的就是我那位兒時玩伴。其實最讓感到驚愕的，還是他蒼白至極的皮膚，以及清癯又閃閃發亮的眸子。他披著又長又亂、如絲質般的頭髮，頭髮繞著臉龐四散地飄開。我甚至難以把他當成一個正常人來看。

P.22

我很訝異這位朋友講話顛顛倒倒的，不過我隨即發現這是因為他想抑制自己的焦慮。對於這種情況，其實我早有心理準備，這不單是由於他的來信內容，也是出自於我兒時的記憶，因為打

從他還是小男孩時，他就有這些身心上的特質了，會忽而好動、忽而沉默。此外，他講話的聲調也會頻頻改變，有時聽起來猶疑、顫抖，有時聽起來又像個酒鬼或毒蟲。

他提起我此行的目的，說他很想見到我，並期待我的出現能為他帶來一些慰藉。這回他話說得很多，還表示他認為這是他們的家族性疾病，所以並不抱希望可以找到治病的良方。

不過他隨即又補充道，那不過是神經方面的小毛病，無疑很快便會痊癒。這種病會有各種異常的官能反應，或許是因為他說話的樣子和態度，他的有些話我聽得都出神了。他深受感官上的過度敏感所苦，所以只能吃些最簡單的食物，並且要穿特定材質所做成的衣物。此外他還發現，任何的花香都讓他覺得受不了，而哪怕再微弱的光線，對他的眼睛都是一種痛苦的折磨，而且只有少數的聲音才不會讓他感到恐怖，其中大多數是弦樂器的聲音他才不會怕。

P.23

疾病

· 艾舍的疾病有哪些外在的徵候？
· 他的症狀有任何怪異之處嗎？
· 你覺得他有哪些地方不對勁？他的疾病是真實的抑或是想像的？請寫下他的疾病會如何影響到他的意識。

他被這種極不正常的恐懼感所掠住。「我會死掉的！我『一

定』會被這種恐懼感嚇死的，一定是被嚇死的。我擔心未來的事情，我不怕危險的事，但事情早晚會發生的，我終有一天會失去性命，失去和這種恐怖的恐懼感搏鬥的理智。」他說。

再透過一些偶而出現的暗示，我又逐漸發現他精神狀態的另一個特色。他對自己所居住的這棟宅院有某種強烈的迷信，而且這種念頭自始至終地糾纏著他，使得他多年以來一直是大門不出、二門不邁。這座擁有灰牆和灰塔的建築，以及映照著這一切的幽暗小湖，長期左右著他的心靈。

P.25

雖然略帶些猶豫，但最後他還是承認，這股哀愁大部分可以追溯一個更原始的源頭——他所疼愛的妹妹患了嚴重的痼疾，而且不久於世了。多年來，這位妹妹不僅是他唯一的伴侶，更是他僅存於世的最後一位親人。「如果連她都走了，」我永遠都忘不了他在說這番話時的哀痛口吻：「那艾舍這個古老家族就只剩下我一個人了。」

當他還在說話時，瑪德蓮小姐（這是他妹妹的名字）正從房間的遠處緩步走過，然後無聲無息地消失，甚至沒有注意到我的存在。我帶著驚訝又有些忐忑不安的心情看著她飄然遠去，我目光發楞地盯著她，不知道該如何形容我當時的感覺。當房間的大門終於在她身後闔上時，我在直覺中又立刻回過頭去看她哥哥，只見他把臉深埋在手掌裡。這時，我還可以看見他瘦削的手指顯得更加蒼白，淚水接著自指縫間潸然而下。

長久以來，瑪德蓮小姐的病情一直讓群醫束手無策。她的症狀頗不尋常，包括對一切都漠不關心、身子骨日益消瘦，常常會陷入深度的昏睡狀態。她至今仍在和病魔纏鬥，但並未纏綿床榻。然而，就在我抵達艾家大院的那天晚上，她終於向病魔投降了（她哥哥在那天晚上以激動不已的心情告訴我這個惡耗）。這時我才明白，我今後再也看不到她的倩影了。

P.26

在往後的幾天時間裡，我們都沒有再提起過她的名字。在這段期間，我竭盡所能地想要讓我朋友的心情好一些。我們一起作畫、一起讀書，或是我在一邊靜靜聆聽他彈著吉他，一切都宛如置

身夢中。不過隨著兩人的逐漸親密，我也逐漸了解到，他的內心世界充滿了灰暗和抑鬱，我想要讓他振作起來的所有努力，都是徒勞無功的。

心情

- 敘事者都伴隨著艾舍做了些什麼事，好讓他的心情好起來？
- 那你呢？心情難過或煩惱時，有什麼可以讓你好受一點？你會做些什麼事來轉換自己的心情？
- 心情低落時，你會去找朋友嗎？還是喜歡自己一個人靜一靜？

　　我和艾家大院的主人就這樣靜靜共度許多時光，這些都將留在我的記憶裡得，但我卻說不清他讓我參與的那些活動。只是不管怎樣，他所即興創作的那些陰鬱音樂，勢必會永遠縈繞我耳際，而他的畫作也讓我戰慄不已，那些生動的繪畫震懾了我，但我不太能解讀這些畫。如果有人能夠藉由繪畫把某個意念完全表達出來的話，那麼那個人一定非羅德瑞·艾舍莫屬。

P. 27

　　朋友的許多作品都呈現出如鬼魅般的幻影，其中一幅由於並不是那麼地抽象，因此我能夠以文字加以描述。那是一幅小小的圖畫，呈現出一條頗為深長的長方形隧道內部，白色的牆面低而平滑。另外這幅圖畫也很清楚的顯示出，這條隧道位置頗深，離地面還有一段距離，完全看不到大門或出口，以及任何的火把或是別的人為光源，但不知道怎

麼卻流瀉出一團強光，讓整幅畫面都沐浴在一片陰森而極不相稱的色調之中。

　　剛才已經提到過，朋友在聽覺神經上的狀況，除了弦樂器所發出的某些特定音調之外，任何的音樂都是這位患者所無法忍受的。或許正是因為他得把自己完全侷限在吉他這麼狹小的範圍內，所以才讓他得以在彈奏時散發出一種奇特的味道，不過這並無法解釋他為何對吉他伴奏的即興詩詞這麼狂熱。在諸多敘事詩的作品中，我還能夠清楚記得其中一首狂詩，而聽他動人的演奏後也給我留下這麼一個印象：看來朋友似乎已經開始查覺到，他馬上就要瘋了。

　　這首即興詩名為《魑魅宮殿》，內容是述說有座充滿珠寶和美好事物的皇宮，精靈們就在琵琶的音樂聲中，圍著國王愉快地跳著舞，而皇宮裡的民眾也以悠美的嗓音唱著歌曲，以頌讚統治者的英明睿智，可是有一天，惡魔卻進入皇宮，殺了國王。那是許多年之前的事了，如今途經那兒的商旅，以及隔著窗子往皇宮裡窺看的人們，都會看見魔鬼們踏著極不和諧的旋律舞動著。

P. 28

　　我記得很清楚，在對這首敘事詩歌的討論過程中，我明白了艾舍所持的觀點，我不太想提到這些是因為它有些標新立異（其他人也跟我有同感），以及他對自身看法的執著。大體而言，他所持的觀點是，即使沒有生命的東西或是物體，也具有感知的能力。這個觀點想必和他對這座祖傳莊園裡那些灰色石頭的看法有關。

在他的想像中，這些感知能力來自石頭塊塊相疊的堆放方式，來自生長在石頭上的苔蘚，來自大宅院四周的枯樹。他補充道，長久以來，這座大宅院和那片死寂湖面所映照出來的倒影，都還未曾被打擾過。

最後他表示，由湖面和牆壁所步步形成的氛圍之中，就可以看到充分的證據來證明這些景物是有知覺的。他說由此所產生的結果很明顯，那便是這股可怕的影響力已鑄造出他家族數個世紀以來的不幸命運，也造就出他現在的這付模樣。他的這番高見不容其他人置喙，我於是三緘其口。

信念

• 艾舍對於周遭的事物以及自己所居住的宅院，究竟持有何種想法？請在正確的欄位裡打勾。
　□ 他覺得宅院的氛圍對自己的家族帶來很好的影響。
　□ 他覺得宅院的氛圍對自己的家族帶來不好的影響。

P.29

我們也一同看了許多書，看來許多年以來，這些書的內容早已盤踞在他的內心深處，佔有重要的一席之地，並且和他的思想息息相關。

我們花了好幾個小時的時間，一起研究一些有關超自然力量、魔鬼信仰和玄學等方面的書籍，例如格雷塞、馬基維利、史威登堡、霍伯格、丹達基內、迪·拉·尚伯、提耶克和坎伯尼拉等人的大作。其中我們最喜歡的是由修道士

伊梅立克·迪·喬隆尼所寫有關於宗教審判的《宗教審判手冊》。我們還讀了一些文章，它們讓艾舍欲罷不能，甚至在拜讀完之後，還會坐在椅子上發呆好幾個小時，其中包括由彭波紐斯·梅拉所寫有關於非洲森林之神和畜牧之神的故事，他們是遠古時期的半人半羊怪物。不過他最大的樂趣，是仔細品味一本十分罕見而奇特的書籍，叫做《教會守靈規儀》，描寫一座被人遺忘的教堂，包括一些為死者而唱的歌曲。

P.30

閱讀

• 你會趁著空閒的時間讀些書嗎？你喜歡讀什麼樣的書？
• 你每個星期會花多少時間在閱讀上？
• 你通常都在什麼地方讀書？和夥伴一起比較一下你們的閱讀習慣。
• 艾舍的閱讀習慣透露了他的哪些事？

有一天晚上，他出其不意地告訴我瑪德蓮小姐去世的消息，然後又表示他打算把妹妹的遺體暫時停放在大宅主牆內的一間地窖內，為期兩個星期，然後再舉行下葬禮，我一聽到這些話，便不由得想起那些書對艾舍所可能帶來的影響。這種處置過程頗不尋常，想必有它的理由，至於到底為何，我就不便妄加議論了。

這位做兄長的告訴我，他是考慮到死者的疾病很特殊，她的那些醫生或許會從中干涉，提出種種有關她病情的問題，再加上他們家族的墓園地處偏遠，而且不夠隱密，在考慮這些諸多因素之後，才做出這個決定。我不否認，我一想到初臨大宅的那天，在樓梯間撞見那位看起來一臉邪氣的醫生之

後，就不再反對這樣的處理方式，我想這也算是一種謹慎下的權宜之計，無傷大雅，即便是有些不近人情也無妨。

P.31

應艾舍之託，我決定親自幫他準備暫厝的相關事宜。當時遺體已經入棺，於是便只有我們倆抬著棺木，來到暫時安放的地點。這時我才發現，安置棺木的這間地窖已經封閉了好長的一段時間，我們的火炬差點被那股密不通風的悶窒空氣給弄熄，也因此我們沒有機會仔細查看一下四周。

地窖十分促狹，濕氣又重，甚至一點光都透不進來，看來它的位置剛好位於我那間臥室正下方的極深之處。顯然在很遙遠的年代裡，這間地窖曾被用來當做地牢使用，或是用做拷打罪犯的房間，後來又當做貯藏火藥或其他易燃物的地方，因為地窖的一部分地板，以及我們剛才所行經的那條長形拱道的整個內部，都被仔細地貼了一層銅箔，另外那道又厚又重的鐵門，也做了類似的防護措施。

P.32

我們把瑪德蓮小姐的棺木放置在地窖內的抬架上，然後將尚未旋上螺絲釘的棺木蓋給挪開一些，好瞻仰死者的遺容。這時我才赫然發現，這對兄妹的容貌竟出奇的神似，簡直就是同一個模子刻出來的，實在有夠嚇人的。艾舍大概猜透了我的心思，於是就喃喃地說了幾句話，這才讓我明白，他和瑪德蓮小姐原來是龍鳳胎。

我們的目光並沒有在死者身上停留太久，因為她那付模樣實在讓人不忍卒睹，還有，讓她在荳蔻年華便香消玉殞的那場疾病，已在遺體的胸口及臉上留下一抹淡淡的紅暈，而嘴角猶掛著一絲費人疑猜的笑意，這些症狀就像平常所看到會讓人呈昏睡狀態的所有疾病一樣。接著我們把棺木蓋蓋緊，上緊螺絲釘，然後關緊那扇鐵門，一路回到大宅院上方的房間。

瑪德蓮小姐的葬禮

P.33

- 當有人過世時，親朋好友通常會有什麼樣的反應？
- 艾舍的妹妹過世時，艾舍的反應如何？
- 瑪德蓮小姐的葬禮有何不尋常之處？
- 對於讓她香消玉殞的那場「疾病」，你有哪些發現？
- 艾舍和瑪德蓮小姐這對兄妹之間，究竟有何特殊的關係？

P.34

在過了幾個痛苦又哀戚的日子之後，原本就有些神智失常的朋友，也開始產生一些明顯的改變。他的日常舉止和態度有了變化，而他平素所留心的那些事情也被他忽略或遺忘。只見他不時地在各個房間來回穿梭，原本就蒼白的一張臉變得更加慘白，眼眸失去了光彩，平時說話的聲調也變了，取而代之

的是畏縮又顫抖的聲音，彷彿心中充滿了極大的恐懼。有好幾次我都認為，他焦躁不安的心在想盡辦法要隱藏一些不可告人的祕密，而且掙扎著想找到勇氣把它給和盤托出。

祕密

- 你覺得保守祕密是很簡單的嗎？你會有無法守住祕密的時候嗎？
- 在什麼情況下把祕密給吐露出來是很得當的？在什麼情況下吐露祕密卻是錯誤之舉？
- 你覺得艾舍的祕密是什麼？

不過有時候，我又認為他被一種難以言喻的瘋狂妄想所苦，因為我曾看見他眼神空洞地凝視著前方，而且長達好幾個小時之久，好像在凝神聆聽著一些幻想中的聲音。難怪那樣的光景把我給嚇壞了，我覺得他心中的恐懼悄悄地感染了我，讓我也感到躁動，愈來愈不安。

P.35

在我們把瑪德蓮小姐的遺體暫厝在地窖後的第七天或第八天晚上，在夜深的上床之際，這股恐懼感掠住了我。我輾轉反側，無法入眠，竭力想釐清我為什麼會陷入這種緊繃的情緒。我想說服自己，這些感覺多半是出自於房間裡那些陰氣沉沉的傢俱，比如那些烏漆抹黑、破破爛爛的帷幕，外面的強風把它們吹得前後飄動，並且把我的床弄得窸窣作響。

然而，我還是無法說服自己。我渾

身不住地打哆嗦，心裡頭有一種很深的恐懼感。我不斷喘著氣，想擺脫心中的那股恐懼。一陣掙扎之後，我靠著枕頭坐在床上。我一面炯炯逼視著滿室的深濃夜影，一面側耳傾聽那一陣陣若有似無的模糊聲響。這些聲音每隔一段時間就會趁著暴風雨暫歇之際，陣陣湧入耳裡。一種難以忍受又無法解釋的強烈恐懼感，緊緊掠住了我。我匆匆披衣起床（因為我想我那晚是無法入眠了），急促地在屋裡來回踱著方步，努力想從剛才所陷入的情境中清醒過來。

我來回踱了幾趟之後，我的注意力便被旁邊樓梯間所傳來的一陣輕微腳步聲給吸引，我認出來那是艾舍的腳步聲。果不其然，沒多久他便輕輕敲著我的大門，提了一盞燈走了進來。此時他的臉色還是像平時那樣，蒼白得有如死屍，但除此之外，眉宇間卻流露出一股狂喜的神色。看來他有股歇斯底里的衝動，只是勉強被自己給壓抑住。他的這種神色讓我有些心煩意亂，但無論如何，這都要比我一個人孤零零地待在這兒來得好，我還鬆口氣地歡迎他的到來。

P.37

「難道你還沒看到嗎？」他先是默默環顧著四周好一會兒，才有些唐突地開了尊口：「你真的沒看到？沒關係，你等一下就會看到。」只見他把提燈小心翼翼地罩好之後，便急忙往一扇窗戶奔去，然後一手推開窗戶，迎向外面的暴風雨。

瞬時之間，陣陣強風不斷的湧入，幾乎讓我們騰空而起。這真是天搖地動、風狂雨驟的一個夜晚，肅殺之氣中透出一股淒美之情。一股旋風正在我們周圍聚起力量，風向不時急劇地改變著。濃密的雲層低懸在大宅院的塔樓上，只見它們急速地翻騰著，天上看不到月亮、星星或閃電。這時，清晰可見的氣體雲層發出奇異的光芒，把天際映照得一片燦爛，籠罩著整座艾家大院。

「不行！你不可以看！」我這樣告訴艾舍，並且略帶粗暴的把他從窗口拉到一張椅子上坐了下來。「這種奇特的景象不過是大自然正常的放電現象，沒什麼好大驚小怪的，這也可能是湖中的沼氣所引起的。我們把窗戶關上，天氣太冷了，對你的身體不好。這裡有一本

你最喜歡的傳奇小說，我來唸給你聽，把這個可怕的夜晚打發掉！」

P.38

我手上的那本舊書，就是朗思洛·甘寧爵士所著的《狂會》，我說這是艾舍最喜歡的作品，其實只是隨口開開玩笑而已，並不是認真的。事實上，這本書的內容又臭又長，不太可能會引起朋友的興趣。只不過，這是我當時所能隨手拿到的書，我只希望我讀的東西，能夠多少紓解一下焦躁不安的艾舍。他要是能聽得投入，就算是裝裝樣子也好，那我的想法也算是奏效了。

P.39

我唸到故事中最為人知的情節，也就是狂會中的英雄人物伊索瑞想要拜訪某隱士的住處，惜緣慳一面，於是打算破門而入。故事的敘述是這樣的：

「伊索瑞生性大膽，如今更仗著七分醉意而變得分外威猛，他不想再繼續等待，想立刻和那位頑固又惡毒的隱士對談。這時，雨水滴落在伊索瑞的肩頭上，他擔心暴風雨馬上就要來到，於是索性掄起大鐵鎚，在門上搗出一個大

洞，硬生生地把開扯裂，再把每一樣東西都給大卸八塊。只聽見木頭發出一陣陣乾裂而中空的聲音，聲勢驚天動地，響遍整片森林。」

P.40

唸完了剛開頭的句子後，我不由得暫停片刻，因為我好像聽到大宅院的某個遠處角落傳來一陣模糊不清的聲響。那是木頭被撕裂和擊碎後所傳出的低沉回音，和朗思洛爵士在書中所描述的景像離奇地相似。但沒多久，我認定這只是想像被激起後所產生的幻覺。毫無疑問地，我不過是湊巧分神了一下，在窗戶所發出的嘎嘎聲響，以及暴風雨逐漸加大後所傳來的尋常嘈雜聲中，那個回音並不足以為怪。我繼續往下唸去：

「好一個大英雄伊索瑞，就這樣闖進了大門，但他卻覓不著隱士的蹤影，讓他又氣惱又意外。取而代之的，他看到的是一隻渾身長滿巨鱗的毒龍，在那兒口吐火舌，蹲守在一座銀地金殿外面，旁邊的牆上懸掛著一面閃閃發亮的銅製盾牌，上面寫著：

進此大門者為勝者
屠此惡龍者得寶盾

伊索瑞掄起鐵鎚，朝著巨龍的腦袋一陣猛打，巨龍在他面前倒地斷氣。巨龍臨死前發出了尖銳可怕的慘叫聲，淒厲無比的聲音使得伊索瑞只得用手摀住雙耳，那種恐怖的聲音是他前所未聞的。」唸到這裡，我再度突然停下來。這一次，我確確實實聽到了遠處傳來一陣低沉的聲響，只是我無法辨別聲音從哪個方向傳過來。那個聲音很刺耳，拖得老長，像是一種很不尋常的嘶吼尖叫聲，簡直和我想像中那條巨龍臨死前的淒厲哀鳴一樣。

這第二次不可思議的巧合嚇住了我，困惑和恐懼的情緒讓我心頭亂紛紛，我力作鎮定，以免神經緊繃的朋友發現異狀後，會擔驚受怕起來。我不確信他是否有聽到那些怪聲音，但在最後幾分鐘時，他的外表和舉止後來確實發生了奇怪的改變。

他慢慢移動地他的座椅，面向房間裡的那扇大門而坐，側臉對著我。我能清楚地看到他的雙唇微微打顫著，像在喃喃自語一般，但沒有發出聲音。他的頭垂在胸前，但我從側面瞥見他的眼睛睜得很大，並未入睡。他的身子不時由這一側扭到另一側，動作雖不大，但和直楞楞的眼神顯得很不搭調。

很快我便注意到這一切情況，於是又重新開始述說朗思洛爵士的故事：
「話說這位英雄擺脫掉狂暴的巨龍之後，便想拿到盾牌，他苦思著如何破解上面的魔咒。他把巨龍的屍首挪到一旁，以免擋住他的路，然後跨過舖了純銀的地板，往牆上的那面銅盾急奔而去，可是還沒等到他走到那兒，銅盾就自動掉落在他腳邊的銀地板上，發出了駭人的震天價響。」

我話一說罷，就聽到了——在那瞬間，彷彿真有一面銅盾重重地摔落在銀地板上。我知道那是中空的金屬所發出的叮噹聲，距離很遠，隱約傳來一股回聲。

感覺

• 你認為敘事者真的聽到了聲響，還是聯想發揮了威力所致？
• 你有沒有碰到這樣的事：明明那地方什麼都沒有，但仍然覺得好像聽到了什麼聲音從那兒傳來？當時是什麼樣的情況？

我嚇住了，整個人跳了起來，然而艾舍卻不為所動，繼續在椅子上來回擺盪。我衝到他坐的椅子邊，只見他雙眼固定不動地向前凝視，面容僵硬如石頭。我把手搭在他肩膀上，卻發現他渾身都在打哆嗦，不斷抖動的雙唇現出一抹陰沉的笑意。我看見他在喃喃自語著，聲音很低、很急促，而且好像絲毫沒有意識到我就在旁邊。我彎下身子靠近他，這才聽清楚喃喃的恐怖話語。

「你還沒聽見嗎？我聽到了，沒

就在他指著大門的那一瞬間，那扇碩大的木門應聲開啟。雖然門是被強風所推開的，可是站在門後的，卻真的是艾舍家族的瑪德蓮小姐。只見她高瘦的身形披著壽衣，白袍上沾著血跡，瘦弱的身軀處處顯現出痛苦掙扎過的痕跡。在一時片刻間，她只是站在門口，身子緩緩地左右搖擺，不住地顫抖著，接著伴隨著一陣低沉的呻吟和哭喊，重重地往她哥哥身上跌去，而就在她要嚥氣的最後一刻，她使勁把哥哥重重地壓死在地板上。他最後如自己所預料的，葬身在恐怖的情景裡。

P. 46

　　我嚇得奪門而逃，當我跨過那座老朽的橋樑時，暴風雨仍瘋狂的肆虐著。這時猛然間一道強光照亮了那條小徑，我回首仰望，想看看這道強光到底是從哪兒射來的，因為身後不是只有那棟宅院以及它的倒影嗎？這時我赫然發現，那道亮光是從紅如鮮血的一輪滿月上所散發出來的，而且正透過那道在過去幾乎無法用肉眼看到的裂縫中照射出來，先前我曾提過，這道裂縫屋頂延伸而下，一直裂到屋子的地基。正當我盯著它猛瞧時，這道裂縫以迅雷不及掩耳的速度往旁邊裂開，裂口一下子整個裂開。我在極度的震驚下，又看到高聳而巨大的牆壁開始崩塌，發出陣陣又長又刺耳的怒吼，那聲音猶如千萬道急流正一古腦地傾瀉而下。沒過多久，那座深沉又陰暗的小湖便靜靜地將艾家大院的斷垣殘壁吞沒了。

錯！我的確聽到了，幾分鐘以前，幾小時以前，好幾天之前，我就一直聽到了！可是我卻不敢說！天啊！可憐可憐我吧！我是個悲慘的人呀！我不敢！我不敢說出來！我們把瑪德蓮下葬時，她還在呼吸！我不是說過我的感覺特別敏銳嗎？現在我告訴你，她第一次在棺材裡移動身子時，我就聽到她的聲音！我在好幾天以前就聽到了，只是一直不敢把它說出來！而到了現在，就是今天晚上……伊索瑞的故事！他一腳踹開隱士的門，巨龍死前的悽慘吼叫，還有盾牌所發出的叮噹聲……還不如說是她破壞棺木的聲音，那是鐵門絞鍊的尖銳聲，還有她在地窖裡不斷掙扎的聲音。我還可以逃到哪裡去？她不是馬上就要來了嗎？她不正急著要來懲罰我的輕率嗎？我聽到了她上樓的腳步聲，聽到了她沉重而可怕的心跳聲！你這個瘋子！」他說到這裡時，突然一躍而起，不要命地尖叫了起來：「你這個瘋子，我告訴你，她現在正站在門外！」

　　他的話彷彿帶著魔咒般的力量，

2 橢圓形肖像

P.58

本書簡介

1842 年,《橢圓形肖像》最初以《Life in Death》的篇名問世,三年後愛倫坡加以編刪,重新以《橢圓形肖像》的篇名出版。這是愛倫坡最短的一篇小說,所述說的仍是其小說慣有的主題:死亡與偏執狂。(偏執狂是妄想症的一種,患者會極度執著於某個想法或情緒)這篇小說的情節,給了王爾德寫《葛雷的肖像》小說的靈感。

《橢圓形肖像》以講故事的方式來述說一則故事。述事者因為負傷,在山區一棟廢棄宅院中找地方過夜,他被睡房中的畫作所吸引,並且看到了一本記錄畫作的冊子。其中有一幅畫像震懾了他,而冊子透露了這幅畫何以如此吸引他。

這個故事以藝術和生命的關係為主題。在小說裡,藝術與生命是敵對的關係。在創作的過程中,對藝術的強烈偏執,有可能攝收人的生命力,最後導致死亡。

過度的執迷(偏執狂)是愛倫坡作品中恆常出現的主題,在前一篇《艾家大院的崩塌》中,主人翁羅德瑞·艾舍最後死於自己的恐懼之中,在下一篇的《紅死病的面具》中,勃培洛王子對紅死病的偏執,最後也導致了自己的死亡。

P. 63

我出意外後,家僕裴卓闖入一間宅院,好讓我有個地方可以遮風蔽雨,不必露天過夜。此處位於亞平寧山脈,我們所找到的這棟宅院很豪華,不過卻陰氣森森的,看起來像是最近不久才被廢棄的。

我們來到一個最小的房間,把自己安頓下來,這間房間的傢俱和擺設不像其他房間那樣奢華,而且是位在比較僻靜的塔樓裡,離主建築有段距離。

這個房間裝潢細緻,但顯得破舊。牆壁上掛著毛織的帷幕,點綴著各式各樣的甲冑武器,還有很多生動的現代畫,裱在飾紋華麗的金色畫框裡。這些畫掛滿了房子的所有主牆,甚至連許多角落裡都有。大概是因為我有點恍神,所以這些畫才特別吸引我的目光。

意外

• 你是否曾經在遠離家鄉時發生意外,或是生了大病?當時發生了什麼事?

• 你覺得敘述這篇故事的人碰到了什麼樣的意外事故?

P. 64

當時已經夜幕低垂,我便吩咐裴卓把房間裡的那些厚重的百葉窗關起來,然後點上蠟燭,再拉開床鋪四周的黑色天鵝絨布幕。我希望這樣一來,即使我睡不著覺,也至少能夠看看這些畫作,或是讀讀在我枕頭上所發現的這本小冊

子，看看裡面是如何詳細探討和描述那些畫作的。

我讀了很長的一段時間，並且凝視著那些畫作，幾個小時的時間就這樣飛快地逝去，轉眼間午夜降臨。我發現燭台的位置不太合我的意，但又不忍喚醒酣睡中的家僕，於是吃力地伸出雙手去移動燭台，以便讓光線能充分地映照在我讀的那本書上。

未料這個動作讓我有了一個意外的發現，大量的燭光這時正落在房間的一個角落裡，照亮了原本一直處於暗處的地方，讓我得以在明亮的光線下，發現一幅先前未曾注意到的畫作。那是一位正值荳蔻年華的少女的肖像。我端詳著這幅畫作，然後閉上眼睛，我不知道自己為何會這麼做。這只是一時衝動下的舉措，而且我也想要確認一下自己沒有看花眼，於是我又再度盯向那幅畫。

P.65

當時我很清醒，可以確信自己眼睛所看到的東西。誠如我先前所說的，那是一幅少女的肖像畫，畫中只出現她的臉部和肩部，在美術的專業領域內，這種畫法稱為「暈映畫」。少女的雙臂、胸部和秀髮的髮梢，都溶入深邃的陰影中，形成整幅畫面的背景。這幅畫的

畫框是橢圓形的，鑲著繁複的金飾，非常華麗。儘管畫框也堪稱為藝術作品，但令人驚嘆的還是畫作本身，只是讓我頗感動容的並非是作畫的技巧，也不是少女天仙般的美麗臉龐，更不是我在恍神之下把她錯看成真人。

我認真地思索著這些特點，在一個小時左右的時間裡，我始終維持著半坐半臥的姿勢，眼睛一眨也不眨地緊盯著畫像猛瞧。最後，直到我認為自己參透了肖像畫的祕密之後，我才躺回床上。

P.66

我發現這幅畫像的魔力是源自於少女的臉部表情，它如此栩栩如生，活靈活現。我初見之際感到很驚愕，接著是一陣迷惑，最後讓我感到害怕。

我帶著深深的敬佩把燭台推回原來的地方。這時，讓我激動莫名的因素逐漸消失，我開始尋找那本討論這些畫作及其歷史背景的小冊子。我翻到專門描述這幅橢圓形畫像的文章，讀到了下面這些內容：

「她是一位美麗動人、快樂盈溢的少婦，不過當她和那位畫家從相識、相戀一直到互結連理後，就開始了她的厄運。這位畫家感情豐富，而且刻苦耐勞，其實在婚前，便『娶』了他的至愛——繪畫。她風華絕代，而且總是開

地笑臉迎人。她熱愛每一樣事物，獨獨痛恨『繪畫』這個情敵。她唯一討厭的東西就是調色板和畫筆等等這些工具，它們搶走了她所愛的人。是故，當她聽到畫家說他想為她畫肖像時，她一陣恐懼。

不過最後她還是順服了，在高塔的一間暗室裡，乖乖地坐了幾個星期，那裡面的光線只能照射到那塊蒼白的畫布。畫家熱愛自己的工作，他時復一時、日復一日，從早到晚馬不停蹄地工作。他是一個狂放不羈又喜怒無常的人，他沉浸在自己的想像裡，沒有注意到新娘子的身心健康都受到了影響。她日益憔悴，任誰都可以一眼看出，只有畫家仍渾然未覺。

P.68

肖像畫

• 你喜歡照像嗎？
• 你會想請別人幫你畫肖像嗎？
• 為什麼這位年輕的新娘並不想被畫肖像畫？

縱然如此，新娘仍繼續展露可愛的笑容，無怨無悔，因為她看到小有名氣的丈夫在作畫中獲得極大的滿足。他日以繼夜地把那位深愛著他的女子繪入畫中，而她卻一天比一天地虛弱。

有些人在看到這幅肖像時，會壓低嗓門地表示這真是一幅讓人嘆為觀止的畫，它展現了畫家對畫中人物的深情。當創作步入尾聲時，畫家不准任何人進入塔樓的這間畫室。

他瘋狂地愛著自己的作品，他的眼光鮮少離開畫布，甚至無暇一顧妻子的臉龐。他沒有看出來，每當畫布上增添幾分色彩，坐在他身旁那位絕美少婦的臉頰上便褪去幾分光彩。

轉眼間就過了幾個星期，畫作已接近尾聲，猶待完成的部分只剩下嘴角一筆和眼睛上刷色。最後，他添上嘴角的一筆，補了眼睛上的顏色。

前一刻，畫家歡天喜地地站在自己的畫作前，但下一刻，他一面凝視著畫作，一面驚懼地開始顫抖起來，面色陣陣慘白。

他放聲大喊道：「看哪！她的確有生命了！」接著驀然望向愛妻——愛妻已經變成一縷芳魂了。

P.67

鬼迷心竅

• 你覺得人們有可能深深著迷於自己的工作、研究或是嗜好嗎？
• 你能想到什麼例子？這種事曾發生在你身上嗎？

3 紅死病的面具

P. 80

本書簡介

《紅死病的面具》於 1842 問世，是一則寓言性的故事，主題和劫數難逃的死亡有關。這篇小說運用了哥德式小說的諸多元素，例如身體與心理上的恐懼感、城堡、封建社會和死亡等主題。

小說中未交代時間和地點，內容描繪一種恐怖的紅死病正在世上迅速蔓延，凡得病者，必死無疑。勃培洛王子和一千位貴族友人遂逃到一個遺世獨立的修道院裡避難，他認為待在那裡就可以安然無恙。

幾個月後，他在多間相連的廂房中籌辦了一場炫目的化妝舞會，每間廂房的裝潢顏色各有不同。最後一間廂房裝潢成黑色，裡頭有一座每個鐘點都會報時的黑鐘。然而就在時鐘敲響子夜的鐘聲時，來了一位打扮成「紅死病」的不速之客。

這則小說是愛倫坡典型的歌德式恐怖短篇小說。在小說中，愛倫坡創造出一種黑暗詭異的氣氛，集中描繪流血與死亡的畫面，「紅死病」的擬人化，為故事增添了超自然的元素。

《紅死病的面具》反映出愛倫坡對短篇小說的看法，他認為短篇小說的創作從頭到尾都應該字字斟酌，各方面都要表現得淋漓盡致。在本篇小說中，強烈的象徵性畫面和流暢的故事鋪陳，編織出一則令人毛骨悚然、卻又深刻表達出人類處境的恐怖故事。

P. 85

「紅死病」肆虐這處鄉間已有一段時日。從來都沒有哪場瘟疫會如此致命與嚴重，從病發到病亡，患者始終置身於腥紅恐怖的鮮血之中。一旦遭受到感染，病患身體就會出現劇痛，並且會突然地頭昏眼花，緊接著大量的鮮血便會從全身毛孔滲出，最後步入死亡。

病發後患者的身體會出現豔紅的斑點，尤其是臉部，這是這種病的必然症狀。這種病的侵襲，只消半個小時就可以奪走性命。

而勃培洛王子是一個無憂無慮、無所畏懼又精明睿智的人，當他發現有一半領地都成了死城之後，便從宮廷召來一千名身強體壯又朝氣蓬勃的騎士與貴婦淑女，一齊前往一座加強了防禦且與世隔絕的修道院避禍。那是一處幅員遼闊又宏偉壯觀的地方，很符合王子那種怪異又不失尊貴的品味。

紅死病

- 為什麼這個病會叫做紅死病？
- 你覺得它是由什麼東西引起的？
- 控制或治療這類疾病的最佳方式是什麼？
- 時下存在著哪些傳染病？我們又是怎樣對付它們的？

只見一堵高聳又厚實的城牆環繞著修道院，其間有數道鐵門，等到大夥兒進門後，奴僕們便以熔爐和大鐵鎚，將大門的門栓焊死。他們決定不留下任何出入的門徑，以防城裡有突發的驚慌失措的狀況。修道院中的糧食飲水不虞匱乏，有了這些未雨綢繆的措施，這些宮廷裡的人就不怕傳染病了，至於外頭的世界，那就自求多福了！

在這當兒，不管是自怨自艾還是胡思亂想，都是愚不可及的，因為王子提供了一切的享樂。逗趣的小丑、解悶的即興詩人、芭蕾舞者、樂師，還有佳人和醇酒。修道院裡應有盡有，又安全無虞，「紅死神」只能在外面興嘆。

這種與世隔絕的生活轉眼就過了五、六個月，雖然瘟疫在外頭猖獗不已，勃培洛王子卻打算辦一場奢華的化裝舞會來款待這一千位友人。

勃培洛王子

- 勃培洛王子是屬於哪一種人？
- 你同意他是個「無憂無慮、無所畏懼又精明睿智的人」的人嗎？
- 他的名字是否有任何特殊的意義？
- 你會選擇到什麼地方去——是和勃培洛王子一起待在修道院裡，還是冒著染上紅死病的危險待在外頭？

這場化裝舞會極盡聲色之娛。我先為各位介紹一下各個廂房。裡面共有七間廂房，形成豪華的組合。在許多皇宮中，廂房會排成長長的一條直線，如果把摺門向兩側的牆邊推開，所有的廂房都可盡收眼底。不過這裡有點不一樣，這也顯示出王子對怪異事物的癖好。

這兒的廂房建造得極不規則，以致於放眼望去頂多只能看到其中的一間，而無法一覽無遺。每隔約莫二十或三十碼，便會出現一個大轉彎，而且每一個轉彎之後，都會出現一番全新的景致。

在左右兩面牆的中間，都立了一扇又高又窄的哥德式窗戶，俯視沿著迂迴曲折的所有廂房而行的密閉迴廊。那些窗戶都鑲上了彩色玻璃，顏色和室內的裝潢極為配搭，比方說最東側的廂房是採藍色系的裝潢，那窗戶的玻璃就採用了更為鮮艷和亮麗的藍色。

第二間廂房的裝飾和繡帷都是紫色的，所以窗戶也鑲了紫色的玻璃；第三間採綠色系，窗戶上也是；第四間以橙色做為傢俱和燈飾的主色；第五間改為白色；第六間是紫羅蘭色；第七間廂房則完全被黑色覆蓋，黑色的天鵝絨繡帷掛滿了天花板，沿著牆壁垂落到地上，在材質與色系都相同的地氈上堆疊出厚重的褶層，然而只有在這個廂房裡，窗戶玻璃的顏色和內部裝飾不同，而是採猩紅色的，如鮮血般的殷紅色。

數字與顏色

- 你的幸運數字是多少？你最喜歡的顏色是什麼？
- 故事中的數字和顏色有何意義？找一位夥伴一起研究，並把你們的看法做一番比較，然後上網找數字和顏色的資訊，認識它們的意義。

P.89

　　七間廂房都沒有燈座或燭檯，因此不會有一絲油燈或燭火的光線從廂房裡透出。不過在沿著廂房而行的迴廊上，每扇窗戶的對面都立了一個沉重的三角架，上面放置一座火盆，熊熊火光會穿透彩色玻璃，把每間廂房照得明亮異常，給人一種色彩繽紛又怪異的印象。

　　在西側的第七間廂房裡，火光透過猩紅色的玻璃映照在黑漆漆的繡帷上，有如鬼魅般，看來可怕極了。凡是走進廂房的人，無不被嚇得臉色慘白，因此沒有幾個人敢踏進裡面半步。

P.89

　　在這間廂房裡，西側的牆壁立著有只黑檀木製的巨鐘，鐘擺左右擺盪著，發出低悶、沉重和單調的滴答聲。當分針在鐘面上轉一圈，準備整點報時之際，這座鐘就會發出一陣清晰、宏亮、深邃又悅耳的音樂聲。不過由於音調實在太怪異了，使得每一個鐘點整的時候，管絃樂團的樂師就得暫停演奏，聽這陣聲響響完，而起舞的賓客也必須暫停舞轉，使得全場的歡樂氣氛都因此而中斷。

P.90

　　當鐘聲還餘音繚繞時，即使最精力充沛的「舞林高手」也會臉色發白，而那些沉著的長者不是一臉疑惑，便是陷入沉思。一旦鐘響的回音完全消失，歡笑聲旋即又會迴盪在整個人群間。

　　此時樂師們會相視而笑，互相嘲弄彼此的神經質與愚蠢，接著一陣耳語，表示下一回鐘響時決不會再被影響到。之後六十分鐘轉眼流逝（才三千六百秒之後），當鐘聲再次響起，大家就又陷入同樣的情緒反應，憂心忡忡、焦躁不安、一臉詫異，一如之前那樣。

P.91

時間

- 你有戴手錶嗎？多久看一次手錶？
- 時間在你人生中的重要性如何？在故事中，時間扮演什麼樣的角色？
- 時間是如何呈現出來的？在時間的主題中，愛倫坡告訴了我們什麼？

　　儘管這些事情層出不窮，但這仍不失為是一場充滿歡樂又奢華無比的盛宴。王子的的品味十分奇特，對於色彩的運用和舞台效果有其獨到的眼光，還有，他的構思大膽而強烈，創意更是狂放不羈和匪夷所思。有些人會覺得他是個瘋子，但他的擁護者並不這樣認為。

　　為了這場宴會，他親自籌劃七間廂房的裝潢和佈置工作，也建議眾、賓客們該如何穿著：外表越是光怪陸離越好。

　　舞池裡炫目燦爛，充滿活力，一派夢幻，到處都可以看到穿著奇裝異服的身影和稀奇古怪的裝扮，猶如瘋子的作品展示。有美麗的、瘋狂的、奇異的、恐怖的，也有令人倒胃口的。

眾人隨著樂團的狂野樂音在七間廂房之間來回穿梭，窗戶所射來的燈光映照著在他們各有奇想的裝扮上。沒多久，立在黑色天鵝絨大廳上的黑檀木巨鐘又開始報時，剎那間，每一樣東西都靜止下來，除了鐘聲，萬籟俱寂。每一位舞者都僵在那兒，而當鐘聲的餘音一消失，大家又嬉笑起來，樂聲也再度揚起，幽幽的人影繼續來回舞動，歡樂更勝先前。然而，大家對第七間廂房仍是裹足不前，不敢越雷池半步。

夜色漸深，一道紅光透過廂房的血紅色玻璃流瀉而下，原本就陰森森的黑色繡帷在照射下變得更恐怖。只要一踏上那漆漆的地氈，耳際就會傳來黑檀木巨鐘的響聲，其聲音肅穆的程度，遠遠超過其他廂房裡那些自得其樂的賓客們所聽到的任何聲響。

化裝舞會

• 你參加過化裝舞會嗎？你裝扮成什麼？你的服裝看起來如何？
• 如果現在就要參加一場化裝舞會，你會想要穿上哪種服裝赴宴？

其他的廂房裡都擠滿了人，生命的心臟在他們體內狂跳著。舞會繼續進行，直到午夜鐘聲即將敲響十二下，音樂和舞者會像之前一樣突然凍結住，也讓沉思者有了更多的時間思索。

就在第十二聲鐘響的嫋嫋餘音消失之前，群眾中有許多人注意到人群中多了一個戴著面具的陌生人物。大家交頭接耳起來，流言蜚語地聊著陌生客的事，形成一陣陣非難的嗡嗡低語，接著變成一陣充滿恐懼驚駭和嫌惡的嘩然。

在我所描述過像這樣一個眾人聚集的場合中，一般的外表都不至於激起這麼激烈的情緒反應，更何況今晚是一場化裝舞會，再怎樣作怪都是被允許的。可是，現在大家所談論的這號人物，卻是那樣的離經叛道，甚至超過了王子所容忍的極限。看來即使是最放浪形骸的傢伙，其靈魂深處仍然會有些心弦是不能隨意碰觸的，否則必引發激烈的情緒反應，還有，有些事物是經不起玩笑的。

所有的人在此刻都一致覺得，這個陌生的傢伙無論是服飾或行徑，都毫無任何幽默的成分或良好的品味。這傢伙又高又瘦，從頭到腳裹著壽衣，遮住臉部的面具可比僵屍的鬼臉，讓人分不清是人是鬼。眾人雖然不能苟同，但或許會隱忍下來，真正過分的是，這名「演員」打扮成「紅死病」的樣子，衣服上還塗著鮮血，寬潤的額頭和整張臉上，更遍佈著猩紅色的可怕斑點。

當勃培洛王子看見這號幽靈般的人物踏著緩慢肅殺的步伐，行經眾人身邊時，起初還因突然間襲來的恐懼和厭惡感而驚顫，但隨即氣憤得漲紅了臉。

「是誰那麼大膽？」王子劃破嘶啞的聲音質問一旁的奴僕：「是誰敢用這

麼藝瀆又不入流的方式來羞辱我們？來人啊，抓住他，扯下他的面具，讓我們看清楚明天日出時要被吊死在塔樓上的傢，伙究竟是何方神聖！」

P.98

陌生人

- 這位陌生人是誰？他有什麼怪異的行徑？你覺得他有何意圖？
- 為什麼他的外表讓人們驚駭莫名？
- 為什麼他讓勃培洛王子怒不可遏？

　　勃培洛王子在開口說話時，人是站在東側的藍色廂房裡，不過由於他勇敢健壯，因此這些憤怒的話語立刻響徹七間廂房，不但宏亮，而且清晰可聞，而樂聲也在他的手勢下戛然而止。

　　王子站在藍色廂房裡，旁邊還侍立著一群面無血色的奴僕。當王子開始疾言厲色地怒斥那傢伙時，這群奴僕便一擁而上，朝著入侵者的方向直奔，未料這時他反而以從容不迫的步伐，往王子那兒一步步逼近，腳步毫無躊躇，大家看得都嚇呆了，竟無一人前去阻止。

P.100

　　一大群人見狀，便好像心有靈犀一般，全都有志一同地從廂房中間往牆邊退去，而陌生人仍踩著從一開頭便顯得與眾不同的步伐，威嚴而平穩地一路穿越色廂房，走進紫色廂房，再經過紫色廂房進入綠色廂房，再穿

越綠色廂房跨到橙色廂房，一路長驅直入，最後經過白廂房而來到紫羅蘭色廂房裡。

　　勃培洛王子這時滿腔怒火，而且為自己剛才一時的懦弱感到羞怒。他一口氣連衝六間廂房，而且大家都嚇壞了，沒有人跟隨在後。王子帶了一把短劍，他迅速傾身向前，離陌生人不到三、四英呎遠，而這時已奔到紫羅蘭色廂房的陌生人突然轉過身來，面對正在追趕他的王子。這時傳來一陣尖銳的慘叫聲，短劍掉落在烏漆抹黑的地氈上，才一眨眼的功夫，勃培洛王子已倒地身亡。

P.101

　　眾人在絕望之下，不知從哪兒召喚來一股瘋狂的勇氣，大家一鼓作氣衝入黑色廂房，想要抓住不速之客，而對方的高瘦身影則靜靜地站在黑檀木巨鐘的陰影下，身子一動也不動。

　　大家倒抽一口冷氣，嚇得張口結舌，因為這時他們發現，在扯掉他的壽衣和如死屍般的面具後，裡面竟然空物一物，沒有人，沒有形體，什麼都沒有。

　　這時大家才明白「紅死病」已經現身，趁著夜色偷溜進來。一個個狂歡的人倒下，嗚呼哀哉，歡宴大廳裡血跡斑斑。黑檀木巨鐘的生命，也隨著最後一位喧鬧作樂的人倒下而劃上休止符。此時，三角架上的火燄已經熄滅，整片大地落入了黑暗、死亡和紅死病的掌心之中。

ANSWER KEY

THE FALL OF THE HOUSE OF USHER

Before Reading

Page 9

4 a) 4 b) 1 c) 2 d) 5 e) 3
7 (Possible Answer) c

Page 10

8 a) 2 b) 5 c) 8 d) 6 e) 1 f) 3
g) 7 h) 4

Page 11

10 1. d 2. f 3. g 4. a 5. b 6. c
7. h 8. e
11 a) lute b) shield c) tapestries
d) tree trunk e) coffin f) web
g) armor h) vault

Page 14

• The narrator and Roderick Usher were
childhood companions.
• Usher writes to the narrator to invite
him to stay with him because he is
unwell.
• Usher asks the narrator to cheer him
up.

Page 16

The Usher family has always been small.

Page 19

(Possible Answers)
• The decaying appearance of the house
and the atmosphere surrounding it.
• The dark and rundown interior.
• The sense of gloom.

Page 23

(Possible Answers)
• He is as pale as a corpse and he has
a shiny look in his eyes. His hair is
wild and everything about him seems
exaggerated. He speaks incoherently.
• He describes his symptoms as being
a heightening of the senses, which
seems to be quite paranoid. He also
says there is no cure but adds that it
will probably go away.

Page 26

The narrator paints and reads with
Usher and listens as Usher plays his
guitar.

Page 28

He thinks the atmosphere of the house
has had a bad influence on his family.

Page 33

• He decides to entomb her temporarily
in one of the vaults of the house.
• Normally people are buried
immediately by professional
undertakers.
• She discovered that her illness had
trance-like symptoms.
• Usher and Lady Madeline are twins.

After Reading

Page 48

7 a) F b) F c) F d) F e) F f) D
g) F h) T i) T j) T k) D l) T

8

mansion/house, malady/sickness,
entombment/burial, physician/doctor,
draperies/curtains, masonry/stones

136

Page 49

9 Summary c) is the most accurate.

Page 50

People who knew Roderick Usher said that he had changed a lot in recent years. They say that his skin was as pale as that of a corpse. His eyes had become large and luminous/shiny. In fact people found the paleness of his skin and the shiny look of his eyes quite startling. His lips were said to be thin and very pale. He had a delicate nose, but his nostrils were broad. His chin was finely-shaped and he had a wide forehead. His hair could be described as silky and soft like a web, but it was also very long and wild. Judging by his appearance he did not seem at all normal

Page 52

17 a) 1   b) 7   c) 6   d) 3   e) 2   f) 4
g) 11   h) 9   i) 10   j) 8   k) 5

Page 53

19 a) 4   b) 3   c) 1   d) 2   e) 5

Page 54

1 1. b)   2. b)   3. b)   4. a)
2 a) 1   b) 3   c) 3   d) 2

Page 55

3

The picture on page 21 depicts the narrator's first meeting with Usher. It's important because it is the first impression that the narrator has of Usher. He notices his friend's strange appearance and nervous reactions. In the illustration we also get a glimpse (in the bottom left) of Lady Madeline. The picture on page 45 shows Lady Madeline's resuscitation during the storm. It is a very dramatic image and we can clearly see the terror of both the narrator and Usher.

Page 56

5 a) 1   b) 4   c) 3   d) 2
e) 1   f) 3   g) 3   h) 2

THE OVAL PORTRAIT

Before Reading

Page 59
3
a) F   b) T   c) T   d) T   e) F   f) T

Page 60
5
a) 2   b) 4   c) 6   d) 5   e) 1   f) 3
6
a) abandoned   b) dreaded
c) deceived   d) surrounded
e) gazed   f) entranced

Page 61
8
1. c   2. a   3. d   4. b

Page 67

She did not want to have her portrait painted because she hated painting because it took her husband away from her.

After Reading

Page 70
6 a) F   b) T   c) F   d) F   e) D   f) D
7

137

a) It refers to the room where the narrator and his servant spent the night.
b) It refers to the painter closing his eyes after he saw the portrait for the first time.
c) It refers to the lifelike expression of the woman in the portrait.
d) This refers to the painting; itself refers to life.

Page 71

9
a) The man, who broke into the house, was the narrator's servant.
b) The painter's old house was abandoned.
c) The narrator read the book that he had found on his pillow.
d) The painter, who was a moody man, was lost in his dreams.
e) The people, who saw the portrait, said it looked like the painter's wife.
f) The young woman, who was once full of energy, became weak and depressed.

Page 72

10 (Possible Answers)

Narrator	Painter	Painter's Wife	Painting
confused	moody	full of energy	alive
delirious	obsessed	fun-loving	admirable
wide awake	wild	humble	lifelike
curious	studious	obedient	startling

Page 73

12 (Possible Answer)
His attitude towards his painting shows his obsession. He worked continuously without noticing that the subject of his painting (his wife) was unwell and dying.

13
a) The painter
b) The people who saw the painting
   The narrator
c) The painter's wife
d) The narrator
e) The painter
f) The people who saw the painting

14 (Possible Answers)
b) The people exclaimed that the painting was very lifelike.
c) The painter's wife insisted that she was fine.
d) The narrator asked Pedro to close the shutters of the room.
e) The painter persuaded his wife to be the subject of his painting.
f) The people declared that the painter was deeply in love with his wife.

Page 74

18 a) 1   b) 5   c) 8   d) 11   e) 9   f) 4
g) 6   h) 10   i) 2   j) 3   k) 7

Page 76

1
a) 1 abandoned   2 mountains
b) 3 servant   c) 4 paintings
d) 5 lifelike   e) pillow

Page 77

4 a) F   b) F   c) T   d) T   e) F   f) F

Page 78

6 a) 2   b) 4   c) 3   d) 2

THE MASQUE OF THE RED DEATH

Before Reading

Page 82

5

a) He is speaking to his friends.

b) A terrible disease is killing everyone.

c) He wants to go to a fortified abbey in the countryside.

d) He takes food and wine with him.

Page 87

• It is called the Red Death because victims bleed from their pores and their bodies are covered with red marks.

• The best way to control or cure diseases like this is to isolate the victims as soon as possible so they don't have contact with other people.

• Medical research, vaccinations and medical drugs are used to help and cure victims of diseases such as AIDS, tuberculosis, yellow fever, malaria and the flu are some infectious disease that exist today.

Page 86

Prince Prospero's name suggests happiness and prosperity (wealth and good fortune).

Page 88

• There are seven rooms in the suite where the masquerade was held. Historically the number 7 is important. According to the bible the world was built in seven days, and there are seven wonders in the world, seven cardinal sins and seven cardinal virtues. In the story seven most likely represents the seven ages of man, and the passage through the rooms the journey from birth to death.

• Colors are also highly significant.

• Red is associated with blood and pain. Black with death.

Page 91

• Time is important in the story. There is a sense of time running out as the disease gets closer and closer.

• It is represented by the beating of the ebony clock, but also by the suite of seven rooms which represent the seven ages of man and therefore man's journey from birth to death. Poe is telling us that we cannot stop time.

Page 98

• The stranger is the Red Death. He walks through the rooms without talking to anyone.

• The guests are horrified because his costume represents a terrible disease.

• Prince Prospero is angry because he says the stranger is making fun of him.

After Reading

Page 102

1 a) A is from *The Fall of the House of Usher*, B is from *The Oval Portrait*, C is from *The Masque of the Red Death*.

2 (Possible Answers)

They are all male. Usher and the Painter are both obsessed by their manias. This obsession eventually destroys them. Prospero and the Painter are both single-minded and determined. They feel as if they are invincible and ignore signs that show otherwise.

3 The narrator gives an outsider's voice and reflects the author's point of view. The narrator is not neutral and judges the behavior of the main characters. The narrator is reliable.

Page 104

10

a) It was a fatal disease and the symptoms were bleeding and red marks.
b) They welded the bolts to make the abbey secure.
c) It was at its worst when Prince Prospero decided to go with his friends to the fortified abbey.
d) He took a thousand friends with him.
e) The fourth room was orange.
f) The guests were dressed in strange and eccentric costumes.
g) They were afraid of the last room because the contrast of the black walls and red light was horrible and gave anyone who entered a wild expression.
h) When the clock chimed everyone stopped what they were doing.
i) He appeared at midnight.
j) The prince was going to stab the stranger with his dagger.
k) He died of the Red Death.
l) They all died.

13 green, blue, purple, black, orange, white, violet

Page 105

14
a) 1 b) 3 c) 8 d) 4 e) 6 f) 7 g) 5 h) 2

15
a) masquerade   b) suite
c) dagger   d) chime
e) pane   f) musicians

Page 106

19 The 'actor' is the Red Death. He is wearing a funeral shroud and looks like a victim of the disease. The partygoers are disgusted because the costume is in very bad taste.

20 His reaction shows his lack of concern for the poor of the country. It also shows arrogance in thinking that thanks to his wealth he can protect himself and his friends.

Page 107

22 We have now been here in the abbey for about five or six months. We have plenty of supplies and tomorrow I will entertain my friends at a masked ball. I will, of course, hold this in the suite of seven rooms that I have personally designed. The rooms are built in an irregular way and each one is decorated in a different color. My favorite room is the black room, which is on the western side. Its color is black and its walls are covered in velvet tapestries of the same color. The windows here are a deep blood/red/scarlet color. The effect this creates is ghastly in the extreme. I'm sure no one will be courageous/brave enough to set foot inside this room. I think I'm going to have a lot of fun.

Page 108

25 (Possible Answers)
a) The seven rooms represent the seven ages of man, and the passage through the rooms represents the journey from birth to death. Seven wonders of the world; seven deadly sins; seven cardinal virtues; according to the bible the world was created in seven days; there are seven heavens and earths in Islamic tradition, etc.

b) The clock represents the inevitability of the passing of time.

c) Prince Prospero's name suggests happiness and prosperity (wealth and good fortune).

d) They are all associated with disguise, not being true to oneself.

26 a) 3   b) 1   c) 5   d) 4   e) 2

`Page 110`

1

a) already   b) who   c) himself
d) was held   e) across   f) hadn't seen
g) as   h) at

`Page 112`

4 a) 2   b) 4   c) 2   d) 4   e) 2

國家圖書館出版品預行編目資料

愛倫坡短篇小說選 / Edgar Allan Poe 著；李璞良
譯 . 一初版 . 一 [臺北市]：寂天文化，2012.4
面；公分 .

中英對照
ISBN 978-986-184-974-4 (25K 平裝附光碟片)

1. 英語　　2. 讀本

805.18　　　　　　　　　　101002383

■作者 _ Edgar Allan Poe　■改寫 _ Janet Olearski　■譯者 _ 李璞良
■封面設計 _ 蔡怡柔　■主編 _ 黃鈺云　■製程管理 _ 蔡智堯　■校對 _ 陳慧莉
■出版者 _ 寂天文化事業股份有限公司　■電話 _ 02-2365-9739　■傳真 _ 02-2365-9835
■網址 _ www.icosmos.com.tw　■讀者服務 _ onlineservice@icosmos.com.tw
■出版日期 _ 2012年4月 初版一刷（250101）
■郵撥帳號 _ 1998620-0 寂天文化事業股份有限公司
■訂購金額600 （含）元以上郵資免費　■訂購金額600元以下者，請外加郵資60元
■若有破損，請寄回更換　■版權所有，請勿翻印